# And I'm Stuck with Joseph

# And I'm Stuck with Joseph

## Susan Sommer

*Illustrated by Ivan Moon*

HERALD PRESS
Scottdale, Pennsylvania
Kitchener, Ontario
1984

**Library of Congress Cataloging in Publication Data**

Sommer, Susan, 1947
    And I'm Stuck with Joseph.

    Summary: Sheila wants a baby sister, but her parents adopt a baby
brother who is very difficult to love.
        [1. Adoption—Fiction.    2. Brothers and sisters—Fiction]    I.
Moon, Ivan, ill.    II. Title.
PZ7.S6965An        1984        [Fic.]        84-611
ISBN 0-8361-3356-0 (pbk.)

AND I'M STUCK WITH JOSEPH
Copyright © 1984 by Herald Press, Scottdale, Pa. 15683
    Published simultaneously in Canada by Herald Press,
    Kitchener, Ont. N2G 4M5. All rights reserved.
Library of Congress Catalog Card Number: 84-611
International Standard Book Number: 0-8361-3356-0
Printed in the United States of America
Design by Ann Graber

84  85  86  87  88  89  10  9  8  7  6  5  4  3  2  1

*For Laura, Christine, Mark, and Jeremy,*
*who taught me what love means.*

# Chapter 1

When my very favorite cousin, Lisa, who's exactly the same age I am, had a new baby sister, I thought that was neat. We're both eleven. And when my other aunt, Norma, had a new baby girl the same week, I began to wish that I could have a baby sister. And when my best friend at school, Julie, had a new baby sister, I asked Mom, "Couldn't we have another baby, too?"

She said, "Sheila Marie Shenk! I think three is enough children for our family."

"Couldn't it just be four?"

"Who do you suppose would have to change all the diapers?"

"I would."

But Mom just laughed. That's the trouble with

my mom. She doesn't believe me. But I *know* I would change the diapers, and change her clothes, and feed her. I used to help Jennifer and David all the time when they were still little enough to let me. Now David's just a yucky brother, and Jennifer's in school, so she doesn't need any help.

And then my very best friend at church, Jill, had a new baby sister too, and she already had two brothers. That made *four* kids in her family. How could Mom and Dad turn me down now? That's when I started praying for a new baby sister. I told God I'd help Mom all the time. I told him I'd change the diapers, even the stinky ones. *Just send me a baby sister, God.*

I got Jennifer to play baby and let me be the mother, so I could show Mom how I could take care of babies.

"I'm the mother, Mom, and Jennifer is my little baby, and you're the grandma."

"I'm not a grandma, yet."

"But you have to be because I'm married and this is my little daughter. And I can change her diapers."

"Sheila, I don't think you should encourage Jennifer to always be the baby."

"Mother."

"You girls go outside and play now. David's out there and he wants to play, too."

"No!" Jennifer said. "Then *he'd* want to be the baby."

My sister's pretty good at getting her own way. If she doesn't want to do something, she just yells "No."

"Well, then," said Mom, "don't play house. Play in the sandbox. Really, Sheila, it's too nice to be inside playing house today."

She didn't get my point at all. Besides, she's always telling us to go outside to play because it's too nice to be inside, but she's inside, isn't she? Isn't that what mothers do? Stay inside to take care of their kids? And who wants to go play with David in the sandbox, anyway? He just wants to play with his tractors and that's baby stuff. *I* want to be grown up and take care of babies.

Then Jennifer started pretending to cry.

"Waa-a, waa. Waa!"

Mom just rolled her eyes. Jennifer is pretty good at sounding like a baby.

"Waa. Waa."

"Aw, come to Mommy, sweetheart," I cooed.

"Sheila, stop that."

Once when our neighbor Mrs. Schmidt was visiting, she thought Mom was babysitting when Jennifer was playing baby.

"Waa. Waa."

"If you must cry like a baby, then go where I don't have to hear you. I've heard enough babies crying for real. I don't need a pretend one around."

See what I mean? Sometimes I don't think my mom cares at all about what I want. *God, don't*

9

*you think you can make her see how much I want a baby sister? I'll help her, I promise.*

One night after supper Dad picked up the paper and started to read when Mom said, "John." She doesn't like Dad to read the paper at the table.

"What?"

"John."

This time she used the tone of voice she uses when she's trying to get him to do something he's forgotten.

"What do you want?"

"Weren't you going to tell the kids something?"

What now? An ice-cream cone? A vacation to Michigan again? Grandma's house?

"Now?"

"Now. When else?"

By now, I knew it was something important, but David kept saying, "Ice-cream cone, ice-cream cone." That's the trouble with five-year-olds. They never know when something really important is coming up.

And Jennifer kept saying, "Let's go to Grandma's, let's go to Grandma's." First-graders aren't much better.

"Hush up, you two," I said, just as Mom took a deep breath like she always takes when things don't go the way she thinks they should.

"John."

"Okay. That's enough. No—no ice-cream cone. We aren't going to Grandma's, and Sheila, let us be the ones to tell them to be quiet."

I was just trying to help.

"All of you, now hush. Sheila, don't look so hurt," said Dad.

"John, will you get on with it?"

"Well, why don't *you* tell them?"

Mom rolled her eyes again, and took another one of her deep breaths and motioned for Dad to go on, and he did.

"*If* we're all ready, then I do have something to say. Your mother and I have decided that here in this old house in the country where we have lots of space, we do have room for another child."

"Yippee!" I said. "We're going to have a baby. I knew it. I knew God would answer my prayer."

"I want a baby sister," said Jennifer, "and Sheila doesn't always get to be the one to take care of her, either."

"I can do it better, can't I, Mom? I've even changed diapers before. I changed David's, and you didn't because you were only one year old then."

"I can too. Mom, let me take care of her, too."

"But I want a brother." David said that. He *would* want a brother to play with his tractors.

"He'd be too little to play with, anyway, David. And you don't know how to change diapers either."

"Mommy, make her let me help, too!"

"Wait a minute. Wait a minute! Children! Whoa!" Dad wanted our attention.

11

So we all got quiet, only David was still talking about a brother, so I told him to be quiet, because we wanted a girl, anyway.

"Sheila, let *us* tell him to be quiet. And don't go into one of your pouts right away. Now, who said anything about a baby?"

"Huh?"

"I said, 'Who said anything about a baby?' "

"You just did. You said we had room for more children and Jennifer and I want a baby sister."

"I distinctly remember saying that in this big old house in the country we have lots of room for another *child*."

"Well?"

"I said child, not baby."

"What do you mean?"

"I mean your mother and I have decided that since we have lots of room, and since we can afford it, and since there are lots of children who don't have homes, we're going to adopt a child."

"Adopt?"

"Adopt," Dad said.

"Mom's not pregnant?"

"Mom's not pregnant."

"A baby?"

"A *child*."

"A sister?"

Mom looked at Dad, then at Jennifer and me, and then at David. Then she said, "Honey, we think it would be nice if David could have a brother. A little boy about three years old would be nice. Then we'd be even, see?"

"What does being even have to do with anything?"

"Well, nothing really. We just thought it would be nice."

"A three-year-old brother?"

"A three-year-old brother."

That's the trouble with parents. You never can figure them out. *God, is this your idea of a joke?*

# Chapter 2

We do live in a big old house in the country, just like Dad said. It's a big two-story white house with enough rooms so that we each can have our own bedroom.

I used to share a bedroom with Jennifer, before Mom and Dad fixed up my room. They put new paper on the walls, and they patched the ceiling, and they refinished the woodwork.

Then I got a new fluffy blue carpet. I knew I wanted blue because that's the color they chose for their room when they put in new carpet. It's soft and warm to sit on when Julie comes over to play. Now it's my very own room, and I don't have to share anymore. I can close the door and nobody, not even Jennifer, bothers me. Even Mom remembers to knock.

Mom and Dad have been doing that with the whole house—patching the ceilings and wallpapering and refinishing the woodwork—ever since we moved here. In fact, Jennifer and David can't remember when we lived in town. They were too little to remember when we moved.

We don't live too far from town now. I can ride my bike into St. Clair on nice days. I have a basket on the bicycle, and sometimes I'll go to the grocery store for Mom. St. Clair, Illinois, has just one grocery store. It's not a very large town at all. It has the school and several churches, but we don't go to church in St. Clair. We drive six miles to Cedar Grove, where there's a Mennonite church. I don't know why. I'd like to go to the Methodist church in St. Clair because that's where Julie goes, but we don't.

"You'll understand better when you grow up, Sheila," Dad says.

I can ride my bike to school, too, in the spring and the fall as long as the weather stays nice. But I usually ride the bus. In the winter it's too cold and icy for bike riding, and on the other days I like to see my friends on the bus.

Our house in the country is back off the road, and Jennifer and I have a long lane to walk every day after school. That's not so bad when the weather is nice. Then I like to see what's going on in the ditch by the lane or in the ditch by the road.

Usually the ditch by the road has empty bottles or cans in it, but sometimes in the summer there are wild sunflowers we can pick, and in the spring after the snow melts, there are rivers in the ditches. Then Jennifer and I can float the empty bottles down the ditch rivers.

In early summer the ditch by the lane has wild strawberries along its bank. Jennifer and David and I can eat as many as we like and Mom doesn't care. She doesn't let us eat as many strawberries as we like when they're from our garden. Then we have to help her pick them and stem them. But we can eat all of the ones by the lane if we want—we just have to beat the birds. They like them too.

And in the fall, just after school starts, and it's still almost too hot to be on the bus, I like to get off the bus and watch the spiders in the crown vetch that's growing on the other side of the lane. The spiders are always huge and black with a bright yellow back. They're hard to see after school, but I always look for them. They're easy to see before school because their webs are covered with dew. That's when the webs are the prettiest. Last year Jennifer and I drew pictures of spiderwebs because we thought they were so pretty.

But in the winter, I don't usually like the long lane. Illinois sometimes gets big snowstorms, and the lane gets so filled with snow that we have to walk in the field. That's when the wind hits hard. If the wind is against my back, I don't mind. But coming home from school, it's in my face. That's when I don't like the country or the lane.

"Don't complain," Mom says every winter. "I used to have to walk clear across town to get to school. That's a lot farther to walk than the lane is."

We have a barn, too, but Dad isn't a farmer. He's a salesman. That's hard for David to understand. He can't imagine why Dad would want to have an office somewhere when he could be farming. Farming is about all David cares about. Dad says we're pretend farmers, since we have a barn and a farmhouse and a garden and some animals.

The animals are what I like best. I think I'm going to be a veterinarian someday. I especially like my own rabbits. I feed them and water them every day, and that was my job then, too.

It was almost the end of summer, just about the time we started noticing the fat spiders in the lane, and the katydids sang us to sleep every night with their *waee, waeeeee.* I think they were telling us to get ready for school. The weather was hot and dry, and we needed rain, but the rain seemed to keep skipping us.

The corn in the fields around the house was just beginning to turn from deep green to golden yellow. The silks had long ago turned deep brown and now were beginning to contrast with the drying husks and leaves. When the wind moved

17

across the field, the leaves rattled so that more than once I thought it was raining, even though the sun was shining and the sky was blue.

I tried not to think of a three-year-old brother and hoped something would happen to change Mom and Dad's mind. We hadn't talked about it too much, and I thought maybe they'd forgotten it.

I went out to the barn to get the eggs and feed my rabbits. The geese hissed when I climbed over the fence, and Alexander the duck came waddling up—but I had on long pants, so I didn't mind.

Jennifer didn't like the geese, and she was afraid of Alexander. To tell you the truth, I don't much care for the geese either, the way they hiss, but they've never pecked me. Alex does. He comes right up and pecks our bare legs which is why I like to wear long pants out to the barn. But I don't care. Even with bare legs, his pecks are just pinches and don't really hurt. Alex was a birthday present for me one year.

But Jennifer screams and runs if he starts after her. Then Alex just runs after her more. But she's quick. Mom and Dad call her a monkey. She can usually scoot into the barn ahead of him, screaming all the time. I don't run, and I don't scream, but I still don't care for the geese. Besides, they aren't my geese—they're everybody's.

We have sheep, too, but they don't do anything

to us since we got rid of the ram. Even Mom didn't go out to the barn without a stick when we had him. The sheep aren't really ours—we just board them for the summer. Then Mom and Dad don't have as much mowing to do. Sometimes, when the farmer brings them, they have lambs with them. We try to catch the lambs, but they're too wild to catch. Mom says to give them a little corn to tame them, but it doesn't work for us. All that does is get the ewes to come, but not the lambs.

Once one of the ewes had a brand-new lamb in our barnyard, and we got to pick it up and hold it. That was really neat. But in about two days it could run so fast, I couldn't catch it anymore. Jennifer could. She and David went out together to catch it, and Jennifer caught it. I guess that's why Mom and Dad call her a monkey. But after a week or two, even she couldn't catch it anymore.

But there weren't any tiny lambs left, and the ram was gone, so the sheep didn't even look at me when I went out to feed my rabbits and get the eggs for Mom. Jennifer and David were playing tractors in the sandbox, so they didn't come help me. They each have a rabbit, too, but I have two rabbits—a buck, Dutch, and a doe, Fluffy. Jennifer and David don't have to feed their rabbits, either, unless they decide to come with me. One time David decided to feed his own rabbit, but he left the hutch open and the rabbit got out and almost got killed. I never forget to close the hutch.

That's why it's my responsibility.

Just as I opened Fluffy's door, I heard Jennifer screaming through the barnyard, and I knew Alex was after her. Sure enough, I didn't even get to her rabbit before she and David were in the barn, slamming the barn door to keep Alex out.

"You can't feed Cottontail!" Jennifer yelled immediately.

"You can't feed Peter, either!"

"Why not?"

"Because that's *my* rabbit, and I get to."

"Me, too."

"You guys forget to shut the door."

"We do not."

"Well, feed your dumb rabbits, then."

Sometimes Jennifer plays with me, and sometimes she plays with David. That day it was David. Then she acts really snotty to me. That's the trouble with those two. Maybe if David had a brother, he'd play with him, and Jennifer would play with just me. That wouldn't be too bad.

So I gathered the eggs. We have ten hens and a rooster. All the hens lay brown eggs except for two of them. One lays white eggs, and one is a fancy one Mom got from a mail-order place. That hen lays blue eggs. I always get to take one blue egg to school each spring for show and tell. The teacher never believes that there is a hen that lays blue eggs until she sees the egg.

I like to gather the eggs unless the hens are sitting on the nest. If they're sitting and don't want to get up, they'll peck you if you try to get the eggs. The hens weren't sitting—it was too late in the summer. They weren't laying too well, either.

"Sheila, wait for me."

It was David. I should have known.

"I want to get the eggs."

"Did you shut the rabbit pen?"

"I'm not a baby, Sheila."

"You are, too. Now don't let the hens out!" But it was too late. One was already out of her pen.

"See, I told you. Now go get it."

"You help me, Sheila."

"You let her out."

"Sheila. Jennifer, you help me."

"I'll hold the door, David. Jennifer, you get behind her, and David, you go on the other side so she doesn't get outside, and she'll hop right back in." And she did, too. I don't know why those hens think they want out of their pen. Once they're out, they get scared and want back in.

I started to gather the eggs, but by that time Jennifer wanted to help too, so I let David and Jennifer get the eggs, and I went back to check the rabbit hutch doors. They were locked. Dad and I had put Dutch, the buck, in with Fluffy a few weeks before, and I was hoping we'd have baby rabbits. I couldn't wait. I love baby animals almost as much as I love baby people. Fluffy was getting fat, so it wouldn't be too long.

Jennifer and David had finished gathering the eggs—five of them—and had put down the

21

bucket to climb into the haymow. They were looking for Sunshine, the cat. I picked up the bucket.

"I'm leaving," I yelled to them.

"We're playing with Sunny." Usually Jennifer would want to come with me so that I'd keep Alex away.

"What about Alex?"

"David and I don't care. David's got on long pants."

"Well, make sure you shut the door, or the sheep will get in."

I took the bucket of eggs and went out past Alex and the geese.

"Hiss away, you old geese," I told them. Maybe a brother wouldn't be so bad. It wouldn't be like a baby, but maybe then Jennifer would play more with me.

That's the trouble with living in the country. All you've got to play with is your sister and brother. And if they want to play together, and play old baby games, then there's no one your own age. Mom and Dad say there's lots of room to play, but I don't want lots of room. I just wish we'd live next door to Julie, my best friend at school.

I took the eggs in to Mom.

"Why the long face?"

"Nothing."

"Oh." She was rolling out a pie crust.

"Well, Jennifer just wants to play with David."

*"Hiss away, you old geese," I told them.*

"I see."

"She never wants to play with me."

"Maybe she got tired of being the baby."

"I let her be the mommy, but she doesn't want to."

"Oh."

"I'm sick of living in the country. Can I do that?"

"What?"

"Roll out the pie crust."

"Sheila, I'm in a hurry." That's another thing about my mom. She's always in a hurry.

"You're always in a hurry when I want to do something."

"Well, I am. Your father will be home soon, and I want to get this in the oven. You can have the scraps."

The mail was at Dad's place at the table, so I started looking through it. There was a picture of a little kid on top. He had blond hair that came below his ears, brown eyes, and he was grinning.

"Who's this?"

"What? Daddy hasn't even seen that yet, Sheila."

"But who is it?"

"That just came this morning. It's Joseph."

"Joseph?"

"Yes."

"Who's Joseph?"

"He's three, and he needs a home."

"Are we going to adopt him?" I don't know

what I was expecting, but that picture really surprised me. This was a real kid, and he had blond hair and brown eyes—Dad would like that. And he was grinning.

"Are we going to adopt him?"

"Daddy and I are going to visit him, and if all goes well, you kids can meet him Sunday."

"Sunday? What about church?" I had told Jill that I would sit by her. Her mom lets me hold the baby sometimes. I didn't want to miss holding Jill's baby sister.

"No church. We'll take a picnic lunch. That's the only way we can work it in, Sheila. Daddy has to be out of town next week for sales meetings."

Joseph. This Sunday. I looked at the picture, trying to imagine that boy as my brother. I couldn't do it. He was kind of cute.

"He needs a haircut, Mom."

# Chapter 3

We had to drive clear across Illinois just to see Joseph. I didn't mind, at least not at first. I liked to look out the car window and try to imagine what it would be like to live in the houses we passed and the towns we drove through.

I liked to look at the fields, too, and try to pick out the rows as the car whizzed by. Since it was the end of the summer, that was harder to do than it was at the beginning of the summer when the corn and beans weren't full grown. Because the corn was full grown and starting to turn gold in some fields, the row patterns were harder to see. The beans were shorter, so it was easier to see the stripes of the rows.

We played the alphabet game, too. But I could

beat Jennifer and David so easily that I didn't think it was much fun. They always said that I cheated, and I knew I didn't. Mom said they were just angry because it was hard for them.

Mom and Dad had seen Joseph once. They had gone with the social worker on Friday. The social worker had been to our house first—just to see if we had enough room for Joseph and a bed for him to sleep in. We did. Our big farmhouse has lots of room, but David wouldn't get to have a room to himself once Joseph came. He didn't care. Mom and Dad had bought new bunk beds for Joseph and David, and David got to sleep on the top.

That didn't seem quite fair to me. "Couldn't Jennifer and I have bunk beds, too?"

"Sheila, we just fixed up your room."

"But I didn't get a new bed."

"Remember how glad you were to have a room by yourself?"

I didn't answer because I knew that part was true. I did like having a room all to myself. Still, a bunk bed would be nice. Then Julie or Jill could sleep overnight without having to sleep on the floor.

Joseph's middle name was John, just like Dad's name.

"I think God must have meant him for us with that name," Mom said.

"We'll see," said Dad.

Why would his name have anything to do with God? I just kept wondering what he'd be like.

27

Maybe he'd let me push him on the swing and take him for walks. Maybe he'd even let me help him get dressed in the morning and tuck him in bed at night.

"And those brown eyes—just like Daddy's." I think maybe Mom was overdoing it a bit.

"What's the matter with blue eyes, Mom?" I have blue eyes, Jennifer has blue eyes, and David has blue eyes. So does Mom. "You have blue eyes."

"Nothing, Sheila, don't be silly. He's just going to fit right in, that's all."

By the time we finally got to Joseph's foster home, Jennifer and David were fighting in the back seat over who got to sit behind Mom, and I was tired of listening to them, and really tired of the alphabet game.

Inside the house, Jennifer and David hid behind Mom and wouldn't talk at all, but Joseph talked enough for both of them. He looked just like his picture—blond hair below the ears, brown eyes, and grinning. His picture didn't show the dimples he had when he grinned, though. He wasn't a bit shy.

"Well, hi," he said.

"Hi, Joseph," Mom said. "I told you we'd be back today to take you on a picnic. Are you ready to go?"

Jennifer and David still hid behind Mom, not talking. I couldn't think of anything to say either.

"Joseph, this is Sheila, Jennifer, and David."

"I know," Joseph said.

How could he know that already?

"Joseph, you better go potty first," his foster mother said.

"Well, I don't have to go."

"You better try, anyway. I had him all dressed up for you, and he had an accident. I think he was just excited about seeing you."

I didn't know three-year-olds still had accidents.

When Joseph was ready to go, we all piled into the car. Joseph sat in front with Mom and Dad.

"I want to sit in the front," Jennifer said immediately.

"Jennifer, don't start that now," Mom said.

"I do. It's not fair."

"You're not a baby."

"He's not a baby, either. I want to."

"Please, Jennifer, we're almost at the park. See if you can find a table by some swing sets."

"I don't want to. I want to sit in front."

Mom didn't answer her, she just took one of her big breaths again. Then she said, "There's the park. Who sees a good picnic place?"

"I see a slide, Mom," I said.

"I see a swing set," said David. "And a sandbox. And a table. Let's stop there, Dad."

"I want to sit in front," Jennifer said.

"You can't sit in front, because I am," Joseph said. "I'm sitting on your mother's lap, so you can't."

Mom just looked at him and took another deep breath. If I'd have said something like that to Jennifer when she was whining, Mom would have told me to be quiet.

"I want to sit up front."

"John, can't you find a spot?"

Dad pulled in under a tree, and opened the door.

"I liked the other place better," David said.

"All of you better get out and do some running," Dad said.

So we got out, and Joseph got out, and I started to take his hand. "Come, I'll show you the sandbox."

"No!" he said. "I can do it myself." And off he ran.

"Go watch him, Sheila," Mom said.

Jennifer climbed onto Mom's lap, and Mom and Dad looked at each other.

The grass in the park was a nice deep green, greener than back home in St. Clair, where we needed some August rain. The sheep in our barnyard had grazed the grass so short that there wasn't much left for them to graze. They had even pushed their fuzzy faces through the gaps in the fence wire to reach the grass on the other side of the fence. When they did that, Mom didn't have to trim along the fence after she was done mowing. It also meant that their pasture was getting scarce. One night Dad threw out a bale of hay for them, and they ran to eat it.

But in the park, the grass was soft and green. I took off my shoes and socks before I headed toward Joseph in the sandbox. David was already in the sandbox. He had brought a toy car with him, and Joseph wanted it right away.

"I want that," he demanded.

"That's David's, but we brought an extra one for you."

David had just gotten that car for his birthday, so I knew he wouldn't want to share it.

"That's okay, Sheila. He can play with it," David said. I couldn't believe he said that. But Joseph didn't want to play in the sandbox any longer. He took the car and headed for the swing set.

"Want me to push you, Joseph?" I asked.

"Well, of course," he said.

But at the swing set he wouldn't put the car down long enough for me to push him, and he was too little to sit in the swing with just one hand holding on.

"Put the car down, Joseph, so you can hang on."

"No! It's my car."

"It's really David's, but he said you could play with it. You have to hang onto the swing, Joseph."

"No. My car."

I didn't argue with him, and somehow he got his arm around one chain of the swing while he held on with the other hand so that I could push him. But I pushed him only once when he started to get off.

"Hey, wait. The swing's moving. Where are you going?"

"I want to get off."

"Wait, and I'll stop it."

As soon as he was off, he went to the next swing and wanted on that one instead. So I helped him get on and put his arm around the chain and gave him a good push, then he wanted off again. He hurried to the third swing and got situated and wanted off after one push. He did that with the fourth swing, too. And he did it with the fifth swing. Then he decided he wanted back on the first one again. By then I was getting tired of pushing him and was pretty glad when Mom called for lunch. He even let me take his hand when we walked over to the picnic table.

"I get to sit by Mommy," Jennifer declared.

"I get to sit by Daddy," David said.

"I'll sit between Jennifer and Joseph," Mom said.

I never get to sit by Mom.

We had peanut-butter-and-honey sandwiches, carrot slices (Jennifer loves carrot slices), apples, and for dessert we had oatmeal cookies. We all like peanut-butter sandwiches, even Dad, and David gobbles his up pretty fast sometimes. But I never saw anybody eat like Joseph. He chomped his sandwich down before David even had half of his gone. Mom gave him another one, and Dad

"Hey, wait," I said. "The swing's moving.
Where are you going?"

33

said, "Slow down, Bud." But the second one was gone before I had eaten my first sandwich, and he wanted another one. Mom gave him an apple instead. He gobbled that up, too. He even ate the core. Then he wanted a carrot, and Mom gave him three. He had those three carrots down, and I was still working on my peanut butter. Then he took another apple. When he was halfway through that, he saw the cookies and wanted one of those, too.

"Finish the apple, first," Mom said. She's a great believer in making us clean up our plates if we want dessert. I've even eaten liver and onions when she had chocolate cake for dessert. But Joseph didn't think too much of that.

"No! I want a cookie." And he threw the apple on the ground.

I guess he didn't know about Mom's rules. Anyway, he'd already had one apple, not to mention the sandwiches and the carrots.

Mom picked up the apple, brushed it off, and handed it back to him.

"Eat the apple first."

He threw it on the ground again. "No! I want a cookie!"

Mom picked the apple up again, brushed it off again, and set it back on the table.

"Mom, he's just a kid," I said. "What's the big deal about an apple?" I was beginning to feel sorry for Joseph. I never could see the sense in having to clean up my plate.

"Sheila, you stay out of this. Joseph, if you don't want to eat the apple, you don't have to eat the apple."

"I want a cookie."

"Oh. Well, then you'll have to finish the apple first."

"No!"

"Well, Joseph, it's your choice. If you want a cookie, you may have a cookie—as soon as you finish the apple."

By then David and Jennifer were eating their cookies. It looked like maybe they'd finish off the cookies if I didn't hurry and eat my apple, so I did. Then I got my cookie. I looked across the park to where the tennis courts were. The courts were filled, and there was a line of other people waiting to use them. I watched the players moving back and forth across the courts after the ball, but I couldn't see the tennis ball. The courts were too far away. A sweat bee lighted on my arm, and I brushed it away. It didn't go very far—it hovered around Joseph's apple waiting for Joseph to give up on it.

Joseph looked at Mom, and he looked at his apple. "I don't want *this* apple. It's dirty."

"Don't eat it."

"I want a cookie."

"Eat the apple."

"It's dirty."

"*You* threw it on the ground."

If you ask me, I think Mom was being kind of

mean. What if he didn't like us? Then what? Who cared about an old apple anyway? He was just a little kid. I brushed the sweat bee away again and tried to look for the tennis ball. All I could see were the rackets flashing in the sun.

Dad didn't say anything. Joseph didn't even seem to notice that Dad was there. Jennifer and David went to play in the sandbox. I thought I could eat the apple for Joseph, except that Mom was looking. Joseph looked at the half-eaten apple, then the cookie, then the apple again. I brushed away another sweat bee. Those bees were getting to be a nuisance. Then Joseph ate the apple. He didn't just eat it—he ate it the way Joseph eats everything. He wolfed it down, core and all, as though he were starving.

"Now can I have my cookie, please?"

I couldn't believe it. He said *please*!

"Of course you may."

"Thank you."

The cookie was gone as fast as his other food. Then he grabbed David's car and headed for the sandbox.

"He needs a haircut," Dad said.

Mom looked up at the trees and took a deep breath.

# Chapter 4

The following week was the first week of school. School started on Wednesday, and I was going to be in the sixth grade. Jennifer was going to be in the first grade. Her teacher was Mrs. Miller, the same one I had had when I was in the first grade. Mom made me promise to sit by Jennifer on the school bus.

"She rode the bus to kindergarten last year. Why do I have to sit with her?"

"That was just the kindergarten bus. This one has all the big kids on it. Remember when you were in the first grade and everything was scary?"

One minute Mom's telling me not to treat Jennifer like a baby, and the next minute she's telling me to take care of her. I didn't want to sit with the first-graders—they always sit in the front of the bus.

"Just for today, Sheila. Or this week, anyway. Just until she gets used to school."

"Nobody ever sat with me, and I got used to it."

"Sheila?"

"Okay. But just for today."

"Thank you, Sheila."

Wednesday was also the day that Mom was going to return to Joseph's foster home to bring Joseph back to live with us. She and David would leave as soon as Jennifer and I got on the school bus. Dad had a sales meeting out of town all day, so Mom and David were going for Joseph while we were in school. Mom told Jennifer and me to walk to Julie's house with Julie after school, and I couldn't wait. I wanted to hold Julie's little sister.

My sixth-grade teacher was Mrs. Rafferty. She was new to the school, so no one knew if she was mean or not. The teacher I had last year, Mrs. Bracy, was really neat. She had long dark hair that she wore clipped back with barrettes, and I loved it. I begged Mom to let my hair grow so I could wear barrettes, too.

"You're going to want it cut by summer."

"No, I won't."

"Sheila, you will. We'll get it so that it finally starts looking nice all grown out, and you'll be begging to have it cut again."

"I won't. I promise."

"Why do you want it long?"

"I want to put barrettes in it."

"We can put barrettes in it now."

"Mom, it's not the same."

"If I say *yes*, will you let it grow all summer?"

"Yes."

"You'll have to wear a cap when we go to the pool."

"I don't care."

"Promise?"

"Promise."

So she let me, and I never complained once all summer about the swimming cap. I didn't like it too well, though—but I didn't tell Mom that.

I had new barrettes for school and a new dress Mom made. I wondered if Mrs. Rafferty would have long hair, too. Would she be nice or mean? Would she be young or old? Would she be my reading teacher, or just my homeroom teacher? Sixth-graders changed classes for some of their subjects. Even if I was in the sixth grade, it was still a little scary. I was kind of glad to sit by Jennifer on the bus.

Mrs. Rafferty had short hair. She wasn't old, but she wasn't as young as Mrs. Bracy, either. She made me sit in the back of the room right by Richard Green. I didn't like Richard. He had on a fancy watch that beeped every hour, and I thought it was dumb.

At least Julie was in the same room. She got to

sit up front by Todd. I liked Todd. He had dark eyes like Dad's and he was real quiet, and he always knew all the answers.

Mrs. Rafferty was really skinny, too. I don't know how she got so skinny, but she was. She reminded me of our hens right after Mom plucked them. With all their feathers gone, they were pretty skinny. And she didn't smile much. She told us all the rules about getting drinks, and when we could leave our desks, and when we could sharpen our pencils—which was never, except before school or after school or recess. We weren't supposed to break the lead, and we were supposed to notice if it was worn enough to sharpen before school.

And she told us that now that we were in the sixth grade, we were responsible. We were responsible for our own things. We were responsible not to have to go to the bathroom during class (as soon as she said that, I felt like I had to go). We were responsible to play nicely on the playground. And we kept the same reading groups as last year, so it turned out that she was my reading teacher and my math teacher. I didn't get to switch classes until social studies and science.

I kept thinking of going to Julie's place after school to see the baby and about Mom getting Joseph, and what it would be like with him for a brother. I thought he'd like the sandbox, and Sunshine (the cat), and our tire swing. I'd even let him pet Fluffy. I hoped Fluffy would have the baby rabbits soon.

Then I realized that the room was kind of quiet, and everyone was looking at me, including Mrs. Rafferty. Richard was grinning, but Mrs. Rafferty wasn't even smiling.

"Sheila?"

"Yes."

"It's your turn."

I didn't have the slightest idea what it was my turn for. I knew my face felt hot—the whole room felt hot. Richard was laughing now, but I still didn't know what it was my turn to do.

"Your summer vacation, Sheila?"

"Yes?"

"What did you like best?"

"Oh." I couldn't think of a thing—not one thing. I couldn't remember anything I'd done all summer—nothing. I just wanted to go to the bathroom.

"Sheila?"

"My rabbits."

"Your rabbits?"

"Yes. My rabbits."

"What about your rabbits, Sheila?"

"Well, Fluffy's going to have babies."

That's all I could think of to say. Richard snickered.

"See if you can pay attention next time, Sheila. Richard?"

And Richard told the whole class about his va-

41

cation to Canada, and how he got to go on a canoe trip, and all about his canoe trip. And just as he was finishing, his watch beeped. What a great first day of school.

At Julie's house, Julie wouldn't let me change the baby's diapers or rock her or hold her. Finally, her mom said, "Let Sheila and Jennifer have a chance, Julie."

So we each got to hold her. She was so tiny and cute. She wiggled, and I know she smiled at me.

"That's just gas," Julie said. Julie thought she knew everything there was to know about babies, but I had helped with Jennifer and David. So what if David was five years old now—I used to help. I know the baby smiled at me. I hardly even got to hold her when Julie wanted her again.

"She's not used to you. You better let me rock her to sleep."

"She's not crying."

"She's not crying now, but she will. She's not used to you like she is to me."

Then she did start crying.

"See?"

"She'll stop."

"Better let me take her. I know how to make her stop crying." So Julie took her, but the baby kept right on crying until Mrs. Frankel took her.

"You girls go play now. The baby needs to sleep."

Why couldn't we have had a baby? Why did Mom and Dad think they had to adopt? Why a

*"Better let me take her," Julie said. "I know how to make her stop crying."*

three-year-old? I wished I could be Julie.

Then I heard Mom's car drive up with Mom and David and Joseph. Julie was anxious to see Joseph, and to tell the truth, so was I.

"This is my new mommy. This is my new mommy," Joseph was saying.

"Isn't he cute, Sheila?" Julie asked.

"This is my new mommy."

"I know, Joseph," I said.

"Well, this is my new mommy."

"So what? She's my mommy, too," chimed in David. David wasn't about to let Joseph think he was the only special one.

"But she's my *new* mommy."

"Boys," Mom said. "Yes, Joseph, that's right."

"How's it going?" Mrs. Frankel asked.

Mom rolled her eyes and took a deep breath.

"Can you come in for coffee?"

"Thanks, but no thanks. Girls, get your things together. I think we'd better head for home. It's been a long day." Mom looked kind of tired, and the day was plenty hot. The first day of school is *always* hot. She pushed her hair away from her face.

But Joseph had other ideas. "I want to drive," he said.

"Move over, Joseph. You can't sit on my lap while I'm driving."

"I want to drive."

"It's too dangerous."

"I want to drive." He was playing with the

steering wheel and reaching for the car keys.

"Move over, Joseph."

He turned on the radio and flipped the heater.

"No! You may not drive. I'm going to drive."

"I want to drive!" He turned on the turn signal and grabbed the gear shift.

"No, Mommy's going to drive. You're going to move over." She picked Joseph up to move him over, but he still held onto the steering wheel.

"*I* want to drive!"

Mom pried up one hand, and took his other hand from the keys, but Joseph reached for the radio knob again, and turned it on full blast.

"I want to drive!"

"You are not going to drive. You are going to sit down. We're almost home, and you're going to sit still until we get there."

By now Joseph was into the other bucket seat, but he reached back for the steering wheel again with one hand, and for the heater with the other.

"I want to drive!" He was really screaming. "You are not my real mommy! I don't like you. You are not my mommy!"

"This car is not going to move until you are sitting in your seat."

"You are not my mommy. I hate you!"

Julie and her mom were waiting for us to leave. "Good luck," said Mrs. Frankel.

I wanted to hide under the car, or crawl under the seat. My face was hot again, and the car was hot.

45

Joseph suddenly sat down on his side of the car—and reached for the glove compartment.

"No," Mom said.

I thought we'd never get home. I thought Joseph would probably sit there and scream forever, *"I want to drive!"* and empty the glove compartment, and turn on the heater.

But he didn't. All of a sudden he stopped and looked back at Jennifer and David and me.

"That's my new mommy," he said.

# Chapter 5

When we finally arrived home, Mom took all of
Joseph's clothes up to David's room. David had to
share his room, but he didn't care because of the
new bunk beds he and Joseph got. David would
sleep on the top where I wished I could sleep.

"We have new beds—see Joseph?" David said.
"And I get to sleep on the top."

"I want to sleep on top."

"No, you can't. You're too little."

"I am not too little. I'm a big boy. I want to
sleep on the top."

"You're too little."

"I'm *not* little."

"Look, Joseph," Mom said, "I'm putting your
favorite blanket right here on your new bed."

"My blanket?"

"Yes, here it is, right on your very own bed. And here's your teddy, too."

Joseph looked at his blanket and grabbed his teddy bear as if he thought he'd never see him again. "Teddy, Teddy, Teddy." He jumped on his bed and bounced up and down.

"That's *your* teddy, in *your* bed. David will be right above you, but this is your bed, not David's. David may not sleep here."

"Just mine."

"Just yours. You may not sleep in David's bed."

"Just mine," he repeated. I guess he forgot that he wanted to sleep on the top bunk. But he kept bouncing on the bed. I waited for Mom to tell him he couldn't bounce, but she was putting his clothes away. At least some of them. She was putting some in a box to give away. I could see why—they were pretty much worn out.

Joseph kept bouncing with his teddy, and I knew he wasn't supposed to be bouncing like that. Once when Jennifer and I were bouncing on her bed, we broke it. Then Mom and Dad both got angry and made a rule about bouncing. Absolutely no bouncing on beds.

"We can't afford to buy new beds or keep fixing old ones," Dad said.

But here was Joseph, bouncing away, and Mom wasn't doing anything about it.

"Sheila, why don't you take Joseph out to see the sandbox?"

*"This is your bed," Mom told Joseph. "It's yours.*
*David may not sleep in it."*

"Me, too," said David.

"Yes, all of you. Joseph hasn't seen the sandbox or the tire swing or the animals. You go show him."

"Let's go, Joseph."

"I'll share my toys." David said that. I don't know why. He's never been that big on sharing with me. He won't even let me touch his tractors. Not that I want to play with his dumb old tractors—but sometimes when it's just rained and the sand is nice and wet and cool on our bare feet, it *is* fun to make roads in the sandbox and fences for fields from the wet sand. Then I kind of wish that I had a tractor that was just mine.

"I want to stay with Mommy," Jennifer said.

"I'll be right there, Jennifer. You go and play."

"No." Jennifer was going to be stubborn again.

"Then you go ahead, Sheila. I'm almost done here, and I'll come with Jennifer in a minute."

So David and Joseph and I went downstairs and outside to the sandbox. Joseph took to it immediately. He took to David's toys, too. In fact, he started grabbing the cars and trucks and tractors until he soon had all of them around him. *Great,* I thought. *Now he's going to claim all the toys. He's going to fight with David, and be mean to Jennifer and me. He's already been naughty in front of Julie and her mom. What next? Why is he here? Where's my baby sister? Why am I stuck with Joseph?*

Sure enough, grabbing all the toys in the

sandbox wasn't enough. He had to have the tractor in David's hand, too.

"I want that."

"Okay, but then I get one of the other ones."

"No! They're mine!"

"Well, I get one. You can't have them all."

"They're mine!" Joseph was screaming.

"I can have *one*. You can't have them *all*. Can he, Sheila?"

"No, Joseph," I said as nicely as I could. "Let David have one. They're everybody's to share. David can have one." So I picked up one of the oldest cars, one Joseph couldn't care too much about, and handed it to David. "Here, David can have this one, can't he?"

Then he bit me!

It wasn't just a little bite, either. He bit me, and he bit hard. I looked at my arm, and it was bleeding. I couldn't help it, but I was crying.

"Mom! Mom!"

Mom and Jennifer were just coming down the back steps.

"Mom, he bit me. He *bit* me!"

"What?"

"He won't share with David, and I was just trying to help, and he bit me, and it's bleeding. He can't bite, Mom. He's not supposed to bite."

School was awful. Richard Green laughed at me, and Mrs. Rafferty thought I was stupid. My best friend got to sit by Todd and wouldn't let me hold her sister. Joseph acted like a spoiled brat in front of Julie. And now this!

"Go wash it off, Sheila. Wash it off good with soap and water—then get a Band-Aid."

"That's it? That's all you're going to do?"

"He needs love, Sheila. He's upset because his whole life is turned around. We have to be patient with him. Try to understand. Sheila?"

"What?"

"Please try."

Well if you ask me, he needed a whole lot more than love. And he needed it on his backside, too.

That night at the supper table Joseph wasn't any better. As soon as he sat down, he started grabbing food.

"Wait a minute. Just a minute, Bud." Dad called both David and Joseph *Bud* all the time. "We've got to pray first."

"What?"

"We pray before we eat around here. We thank God for the food he has given us. Take Mommy and Sheila's hand. Now, we all bow our heads and close our eyes, and we thank God for supper."

Joseph caught on right away. He didn't know the words to the song we sang, but he didn't talk for once.

If he gobbled his food when we first saw him at the picnic in the park, he wolfed it down now. It's hard to describe just how desperately he grabbed his food. Mom said that he inhaled it. Inhale means breathe in. Well, if he had inhaled it, he would have choked, so he couldn't really have inhaled his food. But he sure did stuff his mouth.

We had macaroni and cheese—that's Jennifer's special favorite, and she's as picky an eater as Joseph's a gobbler. We had macaroni and cheese and peas from our own garden. We had picked them way back at the beginning of summer, right after school was out, the same time as Bible school. We picked the peas in the morning, went swimming in the afternoon, and went to Bible school in the evening. That seemed like a long time ago.

Mom didn't want us to eat the raw peas unless we shelled them ourselves. "If you're going to eat them, then shell your own," she'd say. That's because Jennifer and David always wanted to reach into her bowl of shelled peas. Not me. I mean, I *wanted* to, but I knew better. I shelled my own.

Sometimes Jennifer and David and I would go to the garden and pick peas just for a snack. That was fun, too. That was when school was first out, and we had the whole summer ahead of us, and I was still praying for a baby sister.

Now look what we had: Joseph. I thought David was pretty awful for a brother, but he was nothing compared to what I had now—and Mom was telling me to love him! *And* he was gobbling down his food at the supper table like a hog in a hog pen.

Jennifer, who loves macaroni and cheese, was usually the first one done, but not that night.

Joseph had his plate cleaned up, all the peas eaten, his milk drunk and was asking for more things to eat before I had even finished filling my plate!

"Just a minute, Joseph. Slow down and wait for the rest of us," Mom said. "I haven't even had my first bite."

But Joseph couldn't leave well enough alone. He had to scream. He was the screamingest child I ever saw—or heard.

"No! I want some more!"

Mom took a deep breath and looked at Dad. Dad just raised his eyebrows. "Okay, but please slow down," Mom said.

I watched Joseph while he stuffed his mouth full. He used both hands to shove food into his mouth until his cheeks were so full he couldn't stuff any more in. It wasn't really very nice to watch, but I watched anyway because I couldn't believe it. He put another fistful in, and then he choked.

"Mother, watch him!"

"Joseph! Joseph, I told you to slow down, please. Now I'm going to take your plate away until you eat what is in your mouth. Then you can have some more."

I didn't think he could scream with that much food in his mouth, but he managed, all right. He screamed, but he didn't know my mom. Once she says something, she means it—usually. She did that time, anyway, and she didn't give him his plate back until his mouth was empty—which didn't take too long.

We had ice cream for dessert—vanilla ice cream with strawberries on the top. The strawberries were from our garden, too. We loved to help pick them, even though we couldn't eat all we wanted like we could the wild strawberries. Then Mom froze them, and we ate strawberries with ice cream all winter.

But before dessert, Joseph thought we had to pray again. Mom put the ice cream and strawberries on the table, and told Joseph he couldn't eat until everybody had his ice cream. When everyone had been served, Joseph reached up for Mom's hand and my hand and bowed his head just like we'd taught him to do before supper, and said, "Oh, do we have to pray again?"

Then we all laughed. I couldn't imagine that he didn't know about praying before meals, and then that he'd think you had to pray again everytime you got new food. You know what? It was kind of nice to laugh.

But the day wasn't over yet. After supper I went out to the barn to gather the eggs and to feed my rabbits. Jennifer and David were playing with the tractors in the sandbox, and Joseph stayed inside with Mom. Dad was working in the garden, so I was going to the barn by myself again. To tell you the truth, this time I didn't mind at all. Sometimes I just like to be by myself, and this was one of those times.

I wanted to think about all that had happened that day: Mrs. Rafferty calling on me the first day of school, and my not knowing what her question was; Richard laughing at me; Julie's baby sister, so cute and wiggly and cuddly— maybe next time Julie would let me hold her more; Mom coming home with Joseph.

What can I say about Joseph? There he was, a little spitfire. He wouldn't let me hold him or rock him or help him. He didn't even want me touching him, and he bit me, and bit me hard— harder than Alex ever did. And Mom wanted me to have patience with him because he was upset. Upset! My arm still hurt where he bit me. I was upset, but Joseph wasn't trying to love *me*.

The barn was nice and cool after the heat of the day. The barn swallows that used to have a nest on one of the rafters were now lined up outside the barn on the power line. The barn smelled of rabbits and chickens and sheep, and it was a peaceful place to sit and rest.

That's just what I did. I sat down on a bale of hay and watched the barn swallows. I liked best when they left the line, soared up in the air, and then swooped down—sometimes as close as a foot or less off the ground before they would soar up again. I always thought they might crash into the grass, but they never did. On the days when Mom or Dad mowed with the riding lawn mower, the swallows followed the mower around the yard, picking up insects the mower disturbed.

Alex came waddling into the barn and looked at me, quacking. Alexander's eyes are on the sides of his head, not in the front like people's eyes. When he wanted to look at me he had to turn his head so that his bill was pointed away from me. It took me a long time to realize that he was looking at me with his head turned like that.

"Well, Alex," I said. "What are we going to do? Things seem awful mixed up around here."

But Alex just quacked and waddled back out of the barn. I guess he didn't care about my mixed-up life.

I opened the rabbit hutch to get Fluffy's water dish, and I saw a big pile of fur in the corner. Dad had said she'd make her own nest when it was time for her to have the babies. So I reached in and poked the fur around and lifted it up and sure enough, there were baby bunnies in the nest, and she was still having more!

"Fluffy!" I was so excited I almost forgot about the water dish until I bumped it and knocked it over. That made Fluffy jump. Fortunately, the water dish was empty, so I picked it up and filled it, and replaced it in the hutch. Then I closed the door, making sure I locked it. I ran out of the barn, past the geese hissing away, past Alexander and his quacking, and called to Jennifer and David.

"Hey, come here—Jennifer! David!"

"We're playing tractors."

I was so excited I could hardly stand still long

57

enough to yell at them. "But it's Fluffy! She's having babies!"

"She is? Right now?"

"Yes, come on!"

They came running. Jennifer almost forgot to scream at Alex even though he headed straight for her bare legs, and all the geese hissed loudly. We all crowded around the cage, but we couldn't see much, mostly just the rabbit fur Fluffy had used to make the nest, and Fluffy.

"I saw two of them," I said.

"Can we pick them up?"

I tried to pet Fluffy, but she jumped around, startled. So I picked up the fur again, but still couldn't see much. "We better not pick them up. At least not until she's done having them."

Fluffy seemed a little restless, but we were too excited to care.

"Let's get the eggs and then tell Dad."

We hurried as much as we could with the eggs. This time David was careful not to let any of the hens out, and I took the eggs in to Mom as fast as I could without breaking them. Mom was still doing supper dishes, and Joseph was busy with a wooden spoon and a mixing bowl on the floor.

"I'm cooking," he said.

"Fluffy's having babies, Mom!"

"Slow down. Did you gather the eggs?"

"The eggs are right here, but Fluffy's having babies right now!"

"Where are Jennifer and David?"

"They're telling Dad. Then we're going back out."

"You better let her alone."

"Why? I want to see them. I can't wait."

"Honey, you'll scare her, and she might hurt her babies."

"We'll be quiet. I'm going to get Dad." And I headed for the door again.

"You heard me, Sheila. Let her alone until morning. You may have scared her already."

I got Dad, but he said the same thing. "Let her alone until morning."

"Please, Dad, we'll be quiet."

I was thinking of how we'd already been excited and loud in front of the hutch, how I'd tried to pet Fluffy, and how she'd jumped.

"We will, Dad."

"Okay, then, I'll go with you, but you *must* calm down and be quiet."

So this time Dad went out to the barn with us, and Alexander didn't even come close to Jennifer or us. Alexander never bothered Dad. I can't figure that out. Dad says Alex knows we're afraid of him, but I'm *not* afraid of him at all. In fact, I'll chase him and pick him up. He's really my duck, anyway, since I got him for my birthday one year. But Alex didn't come close this time. He just quacked when we walked by with Dad.

In the barn, we ran to the hutch. When Dad got there, he looked in. Then he opened the door and moved the fur a bit. Then he looked down at me and Jennifer and at David without even closing the door. He looked at Fluffy, and stroked her a bit. She jumped again when Dad petted her. "What's the matter, Mother?" he asked softly.

Then he looked back at me and didn't say anything for a long time. I could see through the barn door that the swallows were lined up on the power line again, their orange bellies facing us. I waited for Dad to say something. Finally he said, "They're dead, Sheila. They're all dead. She got scared, and she killed them herself."

I couldn't believe him. I couldn't believe that they were really dead, that God had let them die. What had they done? We hadn't meant to scare Fluffy. Why did the baby rabbits have to die? Why would Fluffy kill her own babies?

All I could think to do was run. I ran out of the barn, and the barn swallows left the power line. I ran past Alex and the geese and the sheep. I ran across the yard and around the sandbox. I ran up the back steps through the kitchen, by Mom with Joseph still playing with a wooden spoon. I ran upstairs to my own room where I could shut the door—and I did shut it.

Then I had no place else to run, so I lay down on my bed and cried. I cried for Mrs. Rafferty who wasn't Mrs. Bracy and who thought I was stupid. I cried for the baby sister I wasn't going to have, and for the baby rabbits that were dead. I cried for Joseph that was here.

I didn't sleep well that night. Joseph kept having nightmares, and just as I'd drift off to sleep, he'd be screaming. I heard Mom get up to go into his room. I heard him screaming again, and yelling in his sleep. I couldn't make out the words, but I heard Mom's voice, too. Then I went back to sleep, and I dreamed of the rabbits, and Mrs. Rafferty, until I heard Joseph screaming again.

This time I heard Mom rocking in the old rocking chair—the one that she used to use when David was still a baby—and singing, and pretty soon it was quiet again. But I couldn't go back to sleep for a long time. I couldn't understand what was happening to our family or where God was. Why would Fluffy kill her own babies, and why would God let her? Why would God send us Joseph instead of a baby sister?

Then I heard Joseph scream again, and I heard Mom get up again. This time I put my pillow over my head to muffle the sound.

# Chapter 6

It was another hot and dusty day at school, and I was glad to get off the hot bus to walk up the lane for home. The strawberries were long gone, and it was so hot and dry that it was hard to see the spiderwebs on the other side of the lane.

As Jennifer and I came closer to the house, we could see Mom folding dry clothes and hanging up wet ones. The ones she was hanging up were all training pants.

"Where'd he get so many training pants?" I asked, almost startling her.

"Oh, hi, Sheila and Jen. Did you have a good day at school?"

"Yes, but where did he get all those training pants?"

"Well, some were his—they came in his box of clothes—and the rest are left over from David. If you're going in, please be quiet. He's taking a nap right now."

"What's for a snack?"

"I don't have anything special. You can have carrots."

Mom always used to have snacks ready for us when we came home from school. Lots of times if the day was really hot, she'd make milk shakes from frozen blueberries or frozen strawberries and milk mixed in the blender. That was what I had been hoping for.

"How about a milk shake?"

"Not now, Sheila."

"I want a milk shake," Jennifer said.

"Oh, girls, please don't start that today."

"Well, then I want a cookie." Jennifer never seemed to know when she was pushing her luck.

"Carrots, Jennifer."

"Cookies!"

"There are no cookies, and I am in no mood for silly arguments this afternoon. If you don't want carrots, go get a tomato from the garden. I've been fighting with Joseph all day, and doing laundry, and I don't want to fight with you girls, too."

Jennifer and I both knew better than to argue any further, but I didn't think my day was all that great either. Mrs. Rafferty still wasn't smiling, and Richard kept making fun of me if I wasn't paying attention. It was hot in school and hot on the bus, and I wanted a milk shake. We didn't ask for Joseph, did we? So why should we have to give up our after-school treats?

I went upstairs to change my clothes, and didn't even bother to get a carrot. Who wanted an old carrot, anyway? Except Jennifer—they're her favorite. I left her as she was peeling her carrot into the sink.

When I went back outside, Mom was folding the rest of the clothes, so I sat down beside her. It seemed like it was the first time I could talk to her alone since we got Joseph.

"Mom?"

"What, hon?"

"Mom, why did we have to adopt?"

Mom took one of her big breaths. "Honey, Joseph needed a home. Daddy and I looked at you and Jennifer and David, and we thought you were pretty special and that we'd like to share what we had."

"So?"

"So?"

"So, couldn't you have had a baby if you wanted more kids?"

"Sheila, we've had babies. We've had three very special babies and their names are Sheila, Jennifer, and David. Now Joseph needs a mommy and a daddy, too. Why should we bring more children into the world when there are so many children here already that need homes?"

"Well, aren't there any babies that need homes?"

"Yes."

"Then why didn't you get a baby? That's what I wanted."

"I know that, Sheila. But then Joseph would still need a home, wouldn't he?"

"What's the matter with his parents, anyway?"

"We're his parents now."

"You know what I mean. Are they dead or something?"

"No, they're not dead."

"Then why don't *they* take care of him? Why do we have to?"

"I'm sure they wanted to, Sheila."

"Then why don't they?" I had a big lump in my throat. I knew if I looked at Mom, I'd cry, so I looked at David and Jennifer in the sandbox. Our world seemed so topsy-turvy all of a sudden. It didn't make sense at all why we should be the ones to take Joseph.

"Sometimes even when parents want to take care of their children, they can't."

"Why not?"

"There are lots of reasons. Some reasons that you won't be able to understand until you're grown up. Sometimes parents don't know how to take care of children right—like Fluffy."

"What do you mean?"

"Well, Fluffy became scared and didn't know what to do, and she killed her own babies. It wasn't because she didn't love them. She just didn't know what to do. Some parents are a little bit like that. They just don't know how to take care of their children."

"You mean Joseph's parents."

"Yes, that's what I mean."

"I wish I were grown up. Then I could have my own baby to take care of."

"All babies grow up to be three-year-olds someday."

"But not three-year-olds like Joseph."

"Sheila, if you're mixed-up and upset, think of what Joseph must feel like. Everything, *everything* is new here and strange and different. He wishes he could go back, too, and can't understand why he can't. He does lots of naughty things just because he's upset. He doesn't like us very well yet, and he doesn't even like himself too well. Can you understand that? He wants to go back to his old home."

"Well, I wish he could. I think his own parents should take him."

"We are his own parents. Daddy and I *are* his parents, and he is not going back, no matter how much you wish he would."

I looked at my arm, thinking, and saw where Joseph had bitten me the day before. The Band-Aid wouldn't stick after I took my bath, so I had taken it off and hadn't bothered to put a clean one back on. I could see the exact place where his tooth had broken the skin, and where the other teeth had left bruises. Even Alexander's bites didn't hurt that much or leave bruises.

I thought of Dad burying the dead rabbits. I hadn't stayed to watch him do it last night, but I could imagine it well enough. I could almost see him take them out of the hutch, see him carrying them out to the pasture, see him digging a hole in the corner by the brush where the red-winged blackbirds sit, and see him putting those tiny babies in the hole, and then covering up the tiny bodies with black Illinois dirt.

If we hadn't scared Fluffy, those rabbits would still be here. What about Joseph's parents? Not his foster parents, not Mom and Dad, but his first parents? What about them? How could a real grownup not know how to take care of his own child? Would Mom and Dad ever forget how to take care of us? Would I know how to take care of my own children when I grew up?

"Mom?"

"Yes."

"What about you?"

"What about me?"

"Would you ever forget how to take care of us?"

"No, Sheila, not ever. I don't know why things happened to Joseph so that his parents couldn't take care of him, but I do know that people who know how to take care of children don't forget."

"Mom, do I have to love him?"

"Oh, Sheila. God's asked us to. When he said,

"Love your neighbor as yourself, he meant Joseph too. But Sheila, God never said it would be easy."

Then Joseph came out of the house, rubbing his eyes. His hair was standing straight up, and he was carrying his blanket in one hand and his teddy in the other. Mom must have taken him to the barber because he had a haircut; it was no longer below his ears. *Dad should like that,* I thought.

"My mommy," he said as he climbed on Mom's lap.

"My mommy, too, Joseph." I thought I'd try to be a big sister to him even if I didn't feel like it.

"Can I push you on the swing, Joseph?"

"No!"

"He's still sleepy, Sheila. Give him time."

Give him time. Sure. So I walked up to the house while Mom held Joseph, swaying back and forth, chanting, "Mommy loves Joseph, Mommy loves Joseph," over and over as though if he heard it often enough, he'd believe it.

I went through the kitchen into the toy room, and there was the dollhouse Dad had made for Jennifer and me last Christmas. It was just the right size for our dolls, not too little and not too big. But something was the matter. All the furniture was out of place. All the doll clothes were out and thrown all over the room, and there were no dolls in the dollhouse. I ran over to the dollhouse and saw the dolls stuffed behind it.

When I picked them up, I saw that every one of them had had their heads taken off and all their arms and legs removed.

"Mother!" I screamed. I was so angry I could hardly turn around. "Mother!" I was so angry I thought I couldn't move at all. All my dollhouse furniture, and the dolls mutilated. "Mother!"

# Chapter 7

After the dollhouse episode, we moved all my dolls upstairs to my room where Joseph was never supposed to go. That may have helped the dolls, but not much else. A month later, I couldn't see much difference in Joseph.

It was the very end of September and the corn by our house had dried out enough to turn completely golden. One day when I stepped off the school bus the corn was gone and our house stood bare and exposed to the road. All that was left in the field were the broken stalks.

Aunt Helen and Uncle Max were coming. Aunt Helen is Mother's sister. She and Uncle Max were moving from the West Coast to Ohio, and they were stopping at our house in Illinois on the way.

Mom was cleaning the house. You'd think that if the house was clean enough for us to live in, it would be clean enough for company, too. But for some reason that isn't the way my mother thinks. When we have company, even if the company is Mom's own sister, the house has to be cleaned. And since Aunt Helen and Uncle Max were going to stay overnight and sleep in Jennifer's room, that meant that even the upstairs had to be clean—including our bathroom, and especially Jennifer's room.

Jennifer is supposed to clean her own room, so it wasn't really fair that I still had to clean my own room with Jennifer in it while Mom cleaned Jennifer's room.

"She has to help me, Mom."

"No!" said Jennifer. "It's not my room, and it's not my mess, and it's not my dirt. Clean your own messy room."

"Well, you're going to sleep in it. Mom's cleaning yours, so you have to help me clean mine."

"I didn't make the mess. I'm not going to help."

"Mother, make her help me."

"It *is* your room, Sheila," Mom said.

"But it's not fair. You're cleaning her room."

"She has to help," Mom said. "Jennifer, come hang up this dress."

"You're doing all the work," I pointed out.

"Sheila, I have no intention of putting up with your bickering today. I have enough to do without listening to you two fight. Jennifer is helping in her own room. You must clean your room good enough for company."

I still didn't think it was fair that I had to come home from school and clean while Jennifer didn't. I shut my door and turned on my radio. Pretty soon Mom knocked on the door.

"Here's the vacuum cleaner. I'm going to go clean your bathroom, but I want to use the sweeper when I'm done there. I still have our room and bathroom and the boys' room to do. I expect you to be done with it by the time I'm ready for it. Then you can dust."

"It's not fair. Jennifer doesn't have to."

Mom didn't answer me, so I stuck out my tongue at Jennifer, but she didn't even see me. She was already dusting her room. I had to admit, it really did look nice and clean. Mom had put on clean sheets, and she'd made the bed much neater than Jennifer could do by herself. Jennifer never can make the quilt go over the pillows and still tuck in under them, too. She either just covers up the pillows so that they look like lumps under the quilt, or she puts the pillows on top of the quilt so that they aren't covered at all. And she always leaves some wrinkles. I know how to cover my pillows and tuck the quilt under them.

I had that done, and my bed was made nicely and the clothes were all picked up. There was nothing on the floor, so I could easily vacuum now. The room did look nice when I vacuumed. The sweeper made the fluffy carpet stand up so that if I walked on it, I could see my footprints. I really liked that carpet—it was just like Mom and Dad's.

What was really unfair was that the boys didn't have to do anything. David had to make his bed, and that was all. Joseph didn't even have to do that. Besides, I knew Mom was going to remake David's bed, because he couldn't even do as well as Jennifer.

Joseph was following Mom around like a shadow, and David wasn't in the house. He didn't even have to stay in to help. He was probably playing in the sandbox. Joseph wouldn't go outside to play with David. He wouldn't go outside with me, either. He followed Mom around, and that's all. When I offered to take him out to play, he'd just say, "No, I don't want to." Unless Mom went out, Joseph wouldn't go out. And when I did convince him to go with me for a little bit, then he'd wet his pants, and I'd have to bring him back in to get changed.

At first, Mom and Dad didn't say anything about his wet pants. Then it got so that every time Mom had to scold him (and that was a lot, let me tell you) he'd wet his pants on purpose. It was hard to go anywhere with him because of his wet pants. Finally, Mom and Dad started scolding him for wetting. I think he wet on purpose—that's the way he was.

Anyway, Joseph was following Mom around, playing with his teddy. That's all he played with, except if Mom was in the kitchen. Then he wanted to cook. Cooking was his favorite thing, even more favorite than his teddy. He always had one of Mom's spoons out and a plastic bowl. The thing was, he got them out even when Mom wasn't around, and he carried them all over the house.

He wasn't happy with just a spoon, either. He wanted everything out of her cooking drawers and all of her pans. He never asked—he just took them. So Mom had to make a rule that he couldn't get into her things. I guess now she knew how I felt about all my dolls being torn apart.

The thing about Joseph was that he couldn't obey the rules. He kept getting into Mom's drawers anyway. It seemed like he was always breaking or destroying what he got into—like my dolls. Mom would tell him no, but as soon as she wasn't looking, back he'd go and do the same thing. That's the way it was with the drawer in the kitchen.

Mom said, "You may not get into my things unless you ask."

And Joseph said, "Okay."

But when Mom went into the other room for something, Joseph headed for the drawer and took out her candy thermometer, and removed the metal clip, and started using the thermometer to stir in an empty bowl. Then he started banging the thermometer on the edge of the bowl. He banged it until it broke. When Mom

74

*As Mom went into the other room, Joseph headed for the
drawer and took out her candy thermometer.*

came back into the kitchen five minutes later, there was the broken candy thermometer.

"Joseph!" I think Mom was losing her cool. "Did I tell you to stay out of my drawers unless you asked?"

"Yes."

"Did you get into my drawer?"

"Yes, but I understand."

"You understand? You understand? *What* do you understand?"

"I understand not to get into your drawer."

"Then, if you understand, I want you to think about it a while."

That meant that Joseph would have to stand in a corner or sit on a chair by himself.

"No! I don't want to think about it!"

Mom didn't even answer. I think she was too angry to answer, but she put Joseph on the chair.

The thing was, Joseph meant it when he said he didn't want to think about it. He got off the chair.

Mom put him back on.

He got off again, screaming all the time— really screaming, "No, I don't want to think about it. I don't want to think about it."

Mom put him back on.

Joseph got back off, still screaming.

Mom put him back on and held him there.

"You *will* sit here."

"No!"

"Yes!" And she made him sit there. She held

him down all the time he was screaming and trying to get up. But Mom wouldn't let him get up. Finally, he quit trying to get up, but he didn't quit screaming. So Mom said, "When you're done screaming, you can get off. Then we'll talk. Not until you're done screaming."

That made Joseph scream even more. But Mom walked into the kitchen and sat down where Joseph couldn't see her. I guess she forgot that I was still there, because I saw her put her hands in front of her face and start to cry. Joseph was still screaming, "I don't want to think about it, I don't want to think about it!" in the other room with Mom crying in the kitchen.

That's the way he obeyed the rules.

But now he was following Mom around with his teddy while she was cleaning for Aunt Helen. I finished vacuuming my room, got the dust rag from Jennifer, and dusted. All my clothes were picked up and all my dolls—moved here after Joseph's damage—were straightened up, and I dusted my desk. My schoolbooks were on the desk, and I remembered that I'd brought home my math to do.

I picked up the math book and looked at the assignment, but couldn't think about it. I kept thinking about Joseph and Mom and Dad. Mom said to give him time. Well, I thought I was. Mom said to be patient, but I don't think Mom was always patient either. Joseph wouldn't even look at Dad, and he never climbed on Dad's lap like

David did. I don't think Dad was always patient either.

Jennifer was at the door, so I put down my math book and told her to come in and we'd play a card game. Jennifer and I both knew that the best thing to do when Mom was cleaning for company was to stay out of her way.

Aunt Helen and Uncle Max came just in time for supper. David and Jennifer and I had been sitting out front waiting for them to drive up the lane. We tried to guess what color their car would be, and how many cars would pass on the road before theirs would turn in. I guessed that they'd have a green car and that it would be the fifth car to come by. Jennifer guessed red and the second car. David guessed white and that they'd be driving a truck.

"Oh, David, just because you like trucks," I said.

"You just wish they'd drive a truck so that you could ride in it," Jennifer added.

"No, sir! They've got to have a truck if they're moving. How else would they bring their furniture?"

For a dumb brother, I had to admit he had a point.

Just then a white car pulled in, and it was pulling a trailer.

"See?" I said. "I told you."

"Well, it's white anyway, so I won."

"No, you didn't. Nobody won."

"I did, I did, and I get to tell Mom they're here."

David dashed off to tell Mom, and Jennifer and I waited to see them get out of the car. They didn't have any children, but they had a cat. He was all black, and his name was Rascal. As soon as Aunt Helen let him out of the car, he ran under it and wouldn't budge, even though Jennifer and I kept calling him.

"I don't think he's used to children," Uncle Max said.

"Just give him some time, girls," said Aunt Helen. "Let's go in and see your mom."

Joseph was sitting on the floor pretending to cook, as usual. The house was really nice and clean, and Mom had the table set, and she even had the good tablecloth on the table. Mom smiled and didn't look at all like she'd been grumpy all day. I don't know how, but my mom can do that. She can be real grumpy, but when the telephone rings, or someone comes to the door or something, she can act like nothing is the matter at all, and smile and even laugh. Sometimes, if it's a telephone call, she'll be grumpy again as soon as she hangs up.

As soon as Joseph saw Aunt Helen and Uncle Max, he jumped up and grabbed one of Mom's legs.

"This is my new mommy."

"And you must be Joseph."

"This is my new mommy."

"Yes, Joseph, I know," said Aunt Helen.

"But this is my new mommy." By this time he had managed to get Mom to pick him up, and he was hanging onto her neck.

"We know that, Joseph. Yes, I am your mommy."

But Joseph wouldn't let anyone else talk. He just kept repeating, "This is my new mommy, this is my new mommy," so Mom and Aunt Helen started talking about the trip anyway.

Then Joseph grabbed Mom's face in both his hands and made her look at him.

"But I thought *you* were my new mommy."

"Oh, honey. I *am* your mommy, and I will stay your mommy. Aunt Helen and Uncle Max are just visitors. They're here to see Mommy and Daddy, not to see you. I am still your mommy. Aunt Helen won't take you away."

Joseph thought that they were coming to take him away, just like we had taken him away from his foster parents. I don't know if he believed Mom or not, but he wouldn't let go of her neck.

Mom said, "Come, let me show you what we've done with the house."

Mom was really proud of our house. I don't know why. It was an old house and had lots of rooms, and Mom and Dad were always working on one of the rooms. First they'd done their own bedroom and put two bathrooms upstairs—one just for them, and one for us. Then they put new wallpaper and new carpeting in their room. Their carpet was light blue and real soft and fluffy. That's why when they did my room, and Mom let me choose the color I wanted, I knew right away that I wanted a blue room with blue carpet just like theirs. Aunt Helen had seen the house before there were any bathrooms upstairs, and before they fixed the kitchen, but she hadn't been here since.

Jennifer and the boys still didn't have nice rooms. Jennifer was next, Mom promised, then the boys, then the hallway. I liked Mom's room and my room, especially the blue carpet, but I liked the new houses some of my friends had better.

Still, Mom wasn't impressed with my arguments for a new house. Not enough room, she'd say.

Now she was showing Aunt Helen and Uncle Max all over the house—even the boys' room where the plaster was broken away from the wall, and the wallpaper was stained and ripped.

"We've got this to do yet," Mom said.

All the time we were talking, Joseph wouldn't let go of Mom's neck, and she just hung onto him, rubbing his back. It made me kind of wish I were little enough to be held, too.

Once supper was over, Dad lit a fire in the fireplace. "First one of the year," he said—and the grownups sat down to talk. Joseph immediately got out his pans and his spoon to cook, and Jennifer, David, and I went into the toy room to play. We were building with the blocks.

Jennifer and I made a huge castle, and David made a road around it for his cars. He said we could use his cars if he could use our castle, so we took turns driving on the block roads around and into the castle. Then Mom came in.

"Is Joseph in here?" she asked.

"Are you kidding? He'd knock down our castle if he were here."

"Sheila."

"Well, he would."

"Has he been here?"

"No."

"You haven't seen him at all?"

I could see that Mom was getting concerned, and I was too.

"I thought he was cooking."

"I did too. We got to talking, and I forgot to watch him."

I started for the door, thinking of the dolls I'd straightened up so nicely in my room, my very own room where Joseph was never supposed to go. I ran up the stairs and into my room, dreading what I would see—but everything was in place. The dolls were still lined up neatly on my bed, and they all had proper heads and arms and legs. My desk was just as I'd left it—the math book still there unopened. Jennifer's blankets and pillow were folded and on the floor ready for bed. Even the cards were still out, but not bothered.

I gave a big sigh of relief. I even felt a little guilty, thinking that my room would have been the first place he'd head. But where was he?

I turned around and went into Jennifer's room. I saw Aunt Helen and Uncle Max's luggage, but I didn't see Joseph. I looked under the bed and in the closet, even though I knew he was afraid of dark places. He wasn't there.

Next I tried the boys' room. Maybe he had crawled into bed and fallen asleep. I'd heard of kids doing that. Fat chance—not Joseph. Mom and Dad couldn't even keep him in bed at night. He wouldn't go there by himself. And he didn't either. Their room was just as empty. He wasn't under the bunk beds and not in their closet either.

Then I thought I heard something across the hall. That meant Mom and Dad's room. So I turned off the light in the boys' room and went into Mom and Dad's room. That was another place we weren't supposed to be—not in their room or in their bathroom, especially if they weren't there.

The light was off in their room but on in their bathroom, and that's where I found him.

"Joseph! Mother!"

I ran to get her, but I had to whisper when I found her because I didn't want Aunt Helen to hear me.

"You better come quick. I found him."

"What now?"

"Just come, you'll see."

Mom took one of her big breaths, the ones she takes when things don't go right, and followed me.

"How bad is it, Sheila?"

I didn't answer her, just led the way. There in her bedroom on her nice fluffy blue carpet, Joseph had pulled down his pants and pooped right on the floor.

# Chapter 8

A month after Aunt Helen and Uncle Max collected their black cat, Rascal, from underneath the car and headed east for Ohio, we started getting ready for the school's annual open house. It was October and most of the corn in the area had been picked. The cornstalks that had remained in the fields by our house had been chopped up and plowed under so that the bare black earth lay in sharp contrast to our still green lawn.

School and Mrs. Rafferty seemed to be fulfilling the promise of the opening day. Mrs. Rafferty never seemed to smile, at least not at me. Julie still was sitting in the front, right next to Todd, and she got A's on all her math papers. I still had to sit beside Richard Green and his beeping watch. Richard made fun of me, snickering every time Mrs. Rafferty called on me, snickering even when I knew the answers to Mrs. Rafferty's questions.

I don't know what he had to laugh about. He may have gotten A's in math like Julie, but he certainly wasn't getting A's on any spelling papers. That was one area where neither Richard nor skinny Mrs. Rafferty could either make fun of me or complain about me.

I had always looked forward to open house. This year I wasn't so sure it was a great thing. I didn't know what papers Mrs. Rafferty would choose to display on the bulletin boards. All the mothers and fathers and even grandparents came to visit the school during open house to see our classrooms, sit at our desks, and visit with the teachers. We have to have neat desks, and the coat closet has to be cleaned up. Even the supply drawers are orderly and neat. All our best work is put on the bulletin boards, and the teachers have us doing extra art projects.

Mrs. Rafferty seemed to be picking on me. She always knew exactly when I wasn't paying attention. And then Richard snickered. Well, I couldn't always help it. I couldn't see the point in all those math problems. We had to do pages and pages of fractions, then we had to go back and check our work. I hated the checks even more than the fractions, and skipped them if I could.

Even if we knew *how* to do the problem and made one teeny mistake, the whole problem was wrong. It was dumb and boring.

It wasn't at all like reading a book. I went to the school library almost every day to check out books. I could read books all day long if people would just let me. The books I read are all happy books, too. If something bad happens, it always gets right again. That's what I like best about books. It seems like the problems I'd read about were easier to solve than my problem—which was basically Joseph. In books, sisters always seemed to love their brothers. I guess that's the way it's supposed to be. Something must be wrong with me somewhere. I mean, even the Bible says, "Love your brother." I don't know how.

I try to love Joseph, but it's just too hard. Every time I start feeling sorry for him, or want to love him, he does something really awful like when he broke my dolls. One day I even told Mrs. Rafferty. That was a mistake.

"Sheila, why are you reading again instead of doing your math?"

That's when I decided to tell her the truth.

"Things always turn out better in books."

"What?"

"It's true, they do."

"What sort of things?"

"Well. . ." Could I trust her? Would she understand? She wasn't smiling, but she wasn't exactly frowning either.

87

"Yes?"

So I took a deep breath and said, "Well, I hate my brothers."

As soon as I said it I knew I'd made a mistake. For one thing, I didn't *always* hate my brothers, especially David. He was okay. Even Joseph I didn't always really hate. I thought of how he hung onto Mom's neck when Aunt Helen came, saying "I thought *you* were my Mommy," afraid that Aunt Helen would take him away from us. And I thought of how we all laughed when he thought he should pray before dessert, and I knew that I didn't really hate him. At least not all the time. But he was so hard to love.

Mrs. Rafferty did not understand at all. I could see it in the shocked look she had on her face. She sucked her breath in quickly and kind of took a step back and said, "Sheila!"

Then I was sorry I'd said anything. I should have just agreed to do my math and forget it.

"Sheila, but we must love our brothers."

Then I didn't know how to make it any better. I couldn't explain about Joseph. I couldn't tell her about how every time I tried to love him, he'd rip apart my dolls or scream that he hates me, or bite me, or poop on Mom's good carpet. I could never tell her *that*. Nobody has brothers that deliberately ruin other people's things. I didn't want her to know that I had a brother who was that bad. And I couldn't explain how that even as soon as I'd said that I didn't love him, I knew it wasn't exactly true either.

I just wanted to run and cry, the way I had run when Fluffy killed her babies. I wanted to run out of the classroom, down the hall, out the front door, and all the way home—up the stairs to my own room, shut the door, and cry. I wanted it all to go away. I wanted our family to be happy like it was before Joseph came. I wished Mom were there right then, but she wasn't. And I didn't know about God either. Hadn't he stuck me with Joseph instead of a baby sister? I didn't even know if I could trust God.

"Sheila, put the book away and do your math. The math must be done before I give you any more library privileges."

So I put the book away and got out the math paper I had to correct. Across the top of the page, Mrs. Rafferty had printed in great big red letters: SLOPPY MISTAKES—*CHECK* YOUR WORK!

"I want you to stay in from lunch recess until you catch up in your math."

Well, I wasn't exactly surprised that she said that, and from the looks of that paper, it would take me all lunch hour to correct my mistakes.

Mrs. Rafferty didn't ask us to write stories very often. Last year Mrs. Bracy let us write all the time, and I always got A's. So when Mrs. Rafferty asked us to write a story before open house, I sat right up and listened carefully to what she had to say.

"I want all of you to write stories, and the best

ones will go on the bulletin board for open house. They can be about anything you want."

It didn't take me long to decide. I wrote a story about a girl named Sandra who had a rabbit that she loved very much named Snowball. Then Snowball had babies and killed them because she was afraid. I thought it was a really neat story. I had Sandra talking to Snowball and everything. I couldn't wait until I got that paper back.

Well, I got it back, all right—all wrong, really. It had a big fat C on it and a bunch of red marks, and across the top of *that* paper Mrs. Rafferty had printed in big letters: THEMATIC TREAT-MENT UNDESIRABLE. I didn't even know what thematic treatment was. I knew that paper wouldn't make it to the bulletin board for open house.

"What's the matter, Sheila, flunk again?" Richard asked.

I couldn't even answer him because I knew if I said anything, I'd cry right there in class. So I just sat staring at my paper and wishing I were home in bed.

That's when Mrs. Rafferty sent a note home with me for Mom and Dad, asking for a conference. I knew then that I must be in big trouble—I must be failing or something. I didn't even tell Julie about it. She showed me her paper right away, and it had a big A on it. I guess she didn't have undesirable thematic treatment. Hers would be on the bulletin board for open house.

"Oh, Sheila," Mom said when she read the note from Mrs. Rafferty. That's all she said. I kind of wished she'd get angry and spank me or something, but she didn't. She just took one of her deep breaths and looked at me.

"I guess I'll go up to my room and read."

"You can't hide from your problems, Sheila."

But I didn't answer her. I went up and lay down on my bed. All day I'd wanted to cry and couldn't because I was in school. Now I was all alone and I had my chance, but I still couldn't cry. *Why are things so mixed up, God? Will they ever get any better?* Then I took out one of my books and read until Mom called me for supper.

The day of open house I cleaned up my desk. Mrs. Rafferty looked at the paper sack I had beside my desk, full of all the junk I was throwing away. It was a big grocery bag Mrs. Rafferty had brought to school just for us to use, and it was completely full.

"Sheila, I can't believe you had all that in your desk!"

"She did, Mrs. Rafferty. It was a real mess." Richard's wasn't all *that* great either, but he'd already thrown his stuff away, so Mrs. Rafferty couldn't see how big a mess he'd had. That was one of the things that made sitting by Richard Green extra difficult.

"Well, I should have just let your mother look at it, I guess."

I didn't say anything, but then I didn't have anything to say either.

"Sheila, try to keep it neat this time."

Well, I didn't *try* to keep a messy desk. It just sort of happened, and I didn't really know how. Besides, mine wasn't any messier than Richard's. Mrs. Rafferty just hadn't seen Richard's.

"Is your math done?"

"Yes."

"Well, I'm putting your last math test on the bulletin board tonight, so that when your parents come, they'll see for sure what you're doing. I don't think all your papers get home."

*Math!* For open house when even grandparents were coming, and everyone would see my grade—couldn't she have picked a spelling test? Now I didn't even want Mom and Dad to come. I didn't want Jennifer or David to come. And I certainly didn't want Joseph to come and show everybody what an awful brother I had. I wasn't looking forward to that evening, but I didn't think I could keep Mom and Dad home.

I tried though.

"Who's going to take care of Joseph when we go to open house?"

"He can go along, Sheila," Mom said.

"Oh, no," I groaned. "He'll mess up all the displays and get into trouble. Can't you stay home with him?"

"I think you know better than that. He has to get used to behaving away from home."

"He doesn't behave at home. Why should he start behaving away from home?"

"That's enough, Sheila," Dad said. "We're all going."

And that was that. Well, I'd tried anyway. Now they would see that math paper, which wouldn't be so bad if the other kids had bad papers up, too. But they didn't. Julie never got any bad papers. She used to be my best friend, but now I wasn't so sure.

Joseph was just like I expected. We started in the first-grade room, and while Mom was looking at Jennifer's desk, Joseph ran to the bookshelf and pulled out all the books. I don't mean some of the books, I mean *all* of the books. They were books from the school library that Jennifer's teacher, Mrs. Miller, had in the room for the kids to read in their spare time. Joseph emptied the shelves.

"Mom! Dad! Get Joseph!"

Dad got to him first and grabbed him by the back of his neck and said, "Bud, you've ten seconds to start putting those books back." Joseph didn't wait ten seconds. He started right then. I've had Dad's hand on the back of my neck before, so I knew why Joseph didn't wait.

I'd had Mrs. Miller in the first grade, too, and I wanted to hide under Jennifer's desk right then. I don't know how Jennifer and David felt. They didn't say anything, but Jennifer doesn't talk too much when she's away from home anyway.

I looked at the bulletin boards in Mrs. Miller's room and remembered when we'd done the same things Jennifer was doing. We'd read the same books and written the same papers and done the same math. All the math was super easy. *Just wait till sixth grade,* I thought. On the bulletin board was a big yellow duckling with a sign beside it saying "Welcome, parents," and all the good spelling papers on it. I found Jennifer's and she'd gotten an A with a big GOOD WORK, JEN-NIFER, on it. Well, my spelling papers were always good, too. But my spelling papers weren't going to be on the bulletin board tonight.

I went back to stand in line with Mom. Jennifer still wasn't saying anything.

Mrs. Miller said, "Well, hi, Sheila. I'm sure glad to see you. I think I'm extra lucky to have had two such nice girls as you and Jennifer. Do things still look familiar to you?"

"Oh, yes," I said. I looked at Mrs. Miller's smiling face and back again to the room I'd had five years before. Then I said something really silly, "I wish I was still in this room."

I guess Mrs. Miller didn't think that was silly—for a grown-up sixth-grader to want to be in the first grade—because she said, "Why, thank you, Sheila. That's one of the nicest things I've heard all day. Mrs. Shenk, you do have two lovely daughters."

"Does Jennifer talk in class at all?" I knew Mom was worried about Jennifer's shyness.

"She does very well, don't you, Jennifer?" Jennifer didn't say anything, but she did smile. I don't know how anyone could be so loud at home and so quiet at school. "She talks when she's called on. She participates in class discussions. She's doing okay."

Mom looked a little relieved. "Thank you, Mrs. Miller. We still have Sheila's room to visit."

Out in the hall I tried one more time. "Mom, I don't want Joseph messing up our room. Why don't we just go home?"

"No, I want to talk to your teacher."

That's what I was afraid of.

In the hall outside the sixth-grade rooms, Mom and Dad stopped to look at the artwork Mrs. Rafferty had displayed. We had made white clown faces and glued them on blue construction paper. We used orange construction paper to make the hair and whiskers. I had cut strips of paper and curled it around my pencil the way we had learned to do it last year in Mrs. Bracy's class, and pasted the curled strips on for hair. Some of the other kids had done the same thing.

"Oh, I see yours, Sheila," Mom said right away. "Look, kids, there it is. Why, isn't that a clever idea, to curl your paper like that? I really like that. You make sure you bring it home so that I can put it up at home."

Maybe the night wouldn't be so bad after all. But Mom and Dad hadn't gone inside the classroom yet. They hadn't seen the math test.

While Mom and Dad were looking at the clowns, Joseph got away. He started running down the hall, yelling, like a little baby runs and yells. He must have thought it was fun to watch us chase him. By the time I'd gotten to him, he managed to turn around and head for my room. He beat me to the door, dashed inside, went directly to the bookshelves that were just like the first-grade shelves, except that the books were harder to read, and emptied the bookshelves before Mom or Dad or I could get to him. I don't know how he got to the shelves so fast, and I don't know how he managed to clear them off so quickly. I couldn't have done it if I'd tried. But it was no problem for Joseph—he did it and turned around and announced, "I emptied the bookshelves."

I didn't even answer him. I just started putting back the books.

"I emptied the bookshelves, Sheila. Ha, ha. I emptied the bookshelves."

I saw Dad heading for him, but so did Joseph. He ran for the coat closet, opened the doors before anyone could get to him, and announced to the world, "I opened up the coat closet."

But before we could reach him, he'd opened up the supply drawers and started emptying them out, too. This time Dad managed to grab him.

Dad didn't say anything—just picked Joseph up and headed for the door. But Joseph said plenty.

"No, don't spank me. I don't want a spanking. I won't do it again. I understand. Am I going to get a spanking? Don't spank me, Dad. I understand. Don't spank me."

They were gone, but not the mess. I had a big lump in my throat again.

"We'll help you, Sheila." Mom put her hand on my shoulder, and David and Jennifer started putting back the books. "You go shut the coat closet and clean up the supply drawers while we do this." It was just as well they had the books to do, so that I could clean up the drawers by myself.

I didn't think I could look at anyone or talk to anyone without crying, and I didn't want to be a baby. So I took my time, putting everything back as neatly as I could. At least Mrs. Rafferty couldn't accuse me of not being neat about the supply drawer. The scissors were all on one side, the rulers beside them. The paste and some construction paper scraps were put back in as carefully as I could do it.

Mom and David and Jennifer finished before I did, and Mom was sitting at my desk reading my papers when I finished. I don't think she had seen the math paper on the bulletin board yet, but I knew it was there.

Mom was reading the story I had written about Sandra and her rabbit Snowball. When she finished, she looked up at me and smiled.

"That's a beautiful story, Sheila." Then she

looked at Mrs. Rafferty standing beside her desk talking to the other parents who had been waiting in line. The line was still pretty long. I hadn't looked at Mrs. Rafferty the whole time Joseph was tearing around, or the whole time I was cleaning up the mess. She was busy talking to parents, so maybe she hadn't noticed the commotion.

Mom put her arm around me. "I guess she doesn't understand about Fluffy."

"I guess not."

Mom looked again at Mrs. Rafferty who was talking to Julie's mother and smiling at her. Then Mom looked back at me.

"Let's go. If she wants to talk to me, I can call her later. It's been a long-enough night."

And we left—just like that, without even saying anything to Mrs. Rafferty. I don't know if Mom or Dad even looked at the math test on the bulletin board.

That night Joseph had nightmares again, screaming, "No, I don't want to think about it!" and "No, don't spank me," in his sleep.

I didn't sleep too well either.

# Chapter 9

The weekend after open house, Joseph learned how to gather the eggs. He'd tried before. He'd tried lots of times. He'd tried the same way he had tried everything else, and he'd always been in trouble.

The first time he had tried to bring in the eggs was the first week he had lived with us. Mom had said he could go out to the barn with us—as long as I was along to watch him—and he really loved it, too. I don't think he had ever seen farm animals up close before.

"You'll have to watch Alexander, Joseph. He likes to bite bare legs. He always goes after Jennifer, so you be careful."

"Who's Alexander, Sheila?"

"Alex is the duck, Joseph."

"Oh, those big hissing things?" he asked pointing to the geese.

"No, silly," David said. "Those are the geese. He doesn't even know what a duck is, Sheila, or what geese are. You'll never be a farmer."

"I will too!"

"No, you won't. Not if you don't know a duck from a goose."

"You didn't *always* know either, David," I said. David really likes to show off how much he knows, especially in front of Joseph. I don't know why he thought he knew so much, just because he could tell ducks and geese apart and name all the brands of tractors. A tractor is a tractor, isn't it? Who cares what make it is or if it's a four-wheel drive or not? At least I don't care.

"I did too always know. I can't remember ever when I didn't know the difference between a duck and a goose."

I decided to ignore him. It didn't matter anyway, because just then Alexander waddled over to us. Jennifer started screaming, and Joseph started laughing.

"*That's* Alexander, Joseph. He's a duck."

"I want to hold him."

"No, he might bite."

But Joseph, naturally, didn't listen to me and took off after Alexander. I thought Alex would hurt him, or the geese would, but they didn't. Alex just took off running—if you can call what a

*Joseph almost caught Alex, but the duck started
flying about six inches off the ground.*

duck does running—with Joseph after him. Joseph almost caught him, too, but Alex started flying about six inches off the ground, and then he could travel faster than Joseph. But that didn't stop Joseph. He kept after Alex until all at once his foot slipped in some sheep manure, and he sat down right in it.

Then we all started laughing. I couldn't help it. It was so funny to see Joseph sitting down in the sheep manure with Alex back down on the ground waddling away, quacking his heart out. I guess Joseph taught Alex a lesson, but then I guess maybe Joseph learned a lesson, too, about running in a barnyard without looking where you're going.

I thought Joseph was going to cry, but when he saw all of us laughing, he broke out in a grin. When Joseph grins he can be about the cutest boy you ever saw, with his big brown eyes and dimples in his cheeks. And he was cute, manure and all, sitting there, grinning.

So I said, "Come on, Pumpkin, let's get the eggs."

Inside the barn, I checked the rabbits while David, Jennifer, and Joseph went into the chicken pen. That was right after Fluffy had killed all her babies. She didn't seem scared to me. She seemed the same as ever, and she let me pet her. Dad said that after she had had time to recover, we'd put Dutch back in with her again, and maybe we would have better luck. So I was petting her and wondering when she would be recovered when I realized that the hens were out again.

"David, you forgot to close the door!"

"I didn't forget. Jennifer was behind me—she forgot."

"I did not. Joseph did."

"Well," I said, "how do you expect Joseph to know to shut the door? Now help me catch them. David you get out here and get over to the far wall. Jennifer, you get by the door, so they don't go outside, and we'll chase them back in."

As usual, the hens really wanted back in, so it wasn't too big a problem getting them back to the pen door, but we had forgotten one thing—one big thing. Joseph. He was still inside the pen, and he thought it would be fun to chase the hens the same way he had chased Alexander. So he took off after them.

"Joseph, no!"

But it was too late—he and they were gone. It was difficult to tell who was after whom. Were the hens after Joseph, or Joseph after the hens? Were we after Joseph, or were we after the hens? I know that *I* was after Joseph.

"Stop it, Joseph, stop it!" I cornered him. "You can't chase the hens like you chased Alexander. They won't lay if they get too excited. And you've let even more out—there's too many out. Now stop and wait right here without moving while we catch them. I mean it—don't move!"

I put him on a bale of hay while we caught the hens. This time it wasn't as simple. Some of the hens had run outside the barn, and first we had to coax them back into the barn before we could convince them to go back into the pen. Jennifer was the best one for outside. If Alex would let her alone, she could dodge around better than David or me, so I sent her out.

Alex let her alone, all right, but the hens weren't convinced that they wanted back into the barn. She chased them completely around the barn three times before she stopped and called for help.

Joseph sat on the bale of hay and screamed, "No! I don't want to sit here. You aren't my boss! I don't want to sit here."

I just let him scream. I didn't have time to answer him anyway. David and I went out to help Jennifer, and Joseph screamed even louder. "Don't let me in here all by myself! I don't want to sit here." But I couldn't help him right then. It was his fault they were out—he was the one who had chased them.

We managed to herd the escaped hens back into the barn. Then we shut the barn door so they couldn't escape again. Inside the barn Joseph was no longer screaming, but his lower lip was sticking way out. When he saw us he said, "But I don't want to sit here."

I still didn't bother to answer him until we managed to get all the hens back into the pen.

Then I turned to him and said, "Don't *ever* chase the hens, Joseph." And I took a big breath. "Now, let's get the eggs."

"Can I come too?"

"Yes, come on. But don't chase the hens."

He joined us in the pen. He eyed the hens, and I thought he was going to chase them again. I quickly shut the door behind him so that even if he did, they wouldn't get out. "Don't chase them, Joseph."

"I won't."

"Then come help with the eggs. You can hold this one." And I gave him a nice, clean brown egg. He held it in his hand and had a big grin on his face. In spite of all the trouble with the hens, I thought he sure was cute with that grin. Then I turned to watch David and Jennifer get their eggs. There were only two more eggs, three with the one Joseph held. The hens weren't laying well that time of year. When I turned to look at Joseph again, the egg he had been holding was lying smashed on the floor. The hens jumped for it immediately. They like egg shells and broken eggs.

Joseph was grinning. "I dropped it."

"I can see that you did."

"I want another one."

"I don't think you can carry it."

"I can. I want another one. Give me another one."

"Will you hold it carefully?"

"I'll hold it carefully, Sheila. I'll be careful. Now give me an egg."

So I gave him the egg David had. I knew if I tried to give him Jennifer's she'd scream. But David didn't care. Then as soon as I gave the egg to him, he threw it on the floor and grinned.

I didn't think his grin was so cute this time.

"That does it, Joseph. No more eggs." To which he promptly started screaming again.

That was the first time Joseph gathered the eggs, and it was the first week he was living with us.

The second time Joseph gathered the eggs, Mom went with us. That time was not too long after the first time. The hens needed more food, and I couldn't lift the feed bag by myself—Mom or Dad always had to fill up the feed tray. Joseph wanted to go along.

"Mom, he deliberately threw down that egg the last time."

"I think he knows better now."

"I know better," Joseph said. "I want to help get the eggs. Let me help, too. I won't throw the eggs."

"Okay, Joseph, but you must hold the eggs carefully."

I looked at Joseph and at Mom, and I didn't think he could do it.

"You didn't see him, Mom."

"Sheila, he has to learn. All the rest of you had to learn, too."

So we went out to the barn. Mom opened the gate, but I climbed over it first. I always thought it was more fun to climb over the gate than to wait for Mom to open it. Sometimes, though, I liked to ride the gate when Mom or Dad opened it. Then they'd swing it way out, and I'd pretend it was a horse. But this time I just climbed over it so that I could beat Mom and Joseph into the barn.

David and Jennifer were playing in the sandbox again. Joseph's coming didn't seem to make Jennifer play with me any more than before. You'd think they'd get tired of tractors. Jennifer does get tired of them sometimes and plays with me. But I don't think David ever does. The only thing he likes better than his toy tractors are real tractors or following Dad around. Dad even lets him drive the lawn mower sometimes, which I don't think is fair at all. He doesn't let me drive it—well, hardly ever. He says it's because I'm not around, that I'm off reading. But I wouldn't be reading if I knew he'd let me drive the lawn mower.

This time I beat Mom and Joseph into the barn and was petting Fluffy by the time they got in.

"Mom, can we put Dutch back in with Fluffy yet?"

"I think it would be all right, Sheila. If she has babies again, honey, I think you'd better remember to be very quiet."

"Mom, I know that by now." Mom is always

reminding me of things I already know. "I think I want to be a veterinarian, Mom."

"That would be wonderful, Sheila. You can be anything you want to be if you want it badly enough to work for it."

"Do you have to know math to be a veterinarian?"

"You have to know math to do almost anything, Sheila. Yes, you'll have to know math to be a veterinarian. And science and biology."

"Are they hard?"

"Sheila, anything can be hard or easy. Sometimes it just depends on whether you want it to be hard or not. If you want to be a vet, you'll be interested enough in science and biology *and* math to study it. Then it will seem easier."

Well, I didn't know about that. It didn't seem to me that anything could make math easier. But still, while I was feeding and watering Dutch and Fluffy, I thought maybe I could do it if I had to do it. But then, being a vet was so far off, I had lots of time to learn math, didn't I?

Mom and Joseph went into the chicken pen. The chicken pen was really an old cow stall. The barn used to be a dairy barn before Mom and Dad bought the farmhouse and the farm buildings. Dad had nailed chicken wire around the stall so that the chickens couldn't get loose inside the barn. The pen had its own door to the outside, and there Dad had fenced in another small area where the chickens could scratch in the dirt and gravel looking for insects. That fenced-in area outside the barn he has also covered with chicken wire, so that even if the hens were outside the barn, they weren't running loose like Alexander and the geese. Chickens can't get through chicken wire, so we always knew where to look for their eggs. The eggs were always in the nest boxes inside the pen in the barn.

I was still feeding Peter and Cottontail, when I heard Mom say, "Here is an egg, Joseph. Now hold it very carefully."

"I will."

"Don't drop it."

"I won't drop it."

I turned around to watch, and Mom started putting the chicken feed into the feed tray. Joseph held his egg carefully. Then he looked up at Mom pouring the chicken feed, and threw his egg on the floor.

"I threw it down, Mom."

"What?" She turned around and put down the feed bag. "What?"

"I threw it down."

"You threw it down?" I don't think Mom could believe he did it on purpose. I could.

"You threw it down on purpose?"

"Yes, but I understand. I won't do it again."

"That's right, you won't. You're not big enough to gather the eggs. Next time you may not carry any eggs. You're not big enough."

Joseph started one of his screaming sessions.

"Yes! I want to. I am *so* big enough!"

"No, I'm afraid not. You're not big enough to get the eggs."

The way he screamed, you'd have thought Mom had spanked him, which is what I would have done—that's for sure.

That was the second time he tried to get the eggs.

The third time Joseph tried to gather the eggs was about two weeks later. Every day when it was time to go for the eggs, Joseph begged to go.

"I am *so* big enough," he'd say. "I won't break the eggs. I know how to carry them carefully. I'm big enough."

"No, you throw them down, Joseph. You're not big enough yet."

Finally, one day Mom said, "You really think you're big enough this time?"

"Yes, I'm big enough. I understand. I won't break the eggs."

"Okay. Tonight you can come with me."

"I'm big enough."

"We'll see, Joseph."

This I had to see, so I went along. In the barn, Mom watched him carefully. I stayed by the rabbits. Fluffy wasn't making a nest yet, but I thought she was bulging at the sides again.

"Here's your egg, Joseph."

"I'll be careful."

"Good. That's being a big boy."

He held the egg carefully the whole time Mom fed and watered the chickens. Mom praised him constantly. After they got out of the pen Mom said, "Look, Sheila, isn't Joseph being a big boy?"

I knew what Mom wanted me to say, so I said it.

"Yes, he is, Mom. He's being a big boy."

Then Mom came over to look at the rabbits, and we both heard the unmistakable splat of an egg hitting the cement barn floor.

"Joseph!" we both said at once.

"I threw it down."

"You little stinker!"

"But I understand. I won't do it again."

Mom wasn't listening to his excuses this time. She grabbed him and pulled down his pants right there in the barn and spanked his bare bottom. Joseph didn't get eggs for breakfast that week.

That was the third time Joseph tried to gather the eggs.

The fourth time Joseph tried to gather the eggs, he went with Dad. That was the day after open house at school, and Dad wasn't all that happy with Joseph, anyway.

"He's old enough to learn how to carry the eggs."

"John, maybe we just shouldn't let him."

"If he's old enough to deliberately throw them down, then he's old enough to be careful deliberately. Come on, Joseph. You're going with me."

This time Joseph wasn't so sure. "I don't want to go."

"Yes, you do. Come on."

Joseph didn't have any choice. He was going with Dad.

"Can I come and feed my rabbits?" I certainly didn't want to miss this.

"Come along."

So off we went to the barn again.

In the chicken pen, Dad held out an egg to Joseph.

"Now, young man, you hold this egg, and you hold it carefully. I want it for my breakfast in the morning. Do you understand that?"

"I understand, Dad. I won't break it."

Dad just looked at him.

"I understand, I said."

"Then here's the egg."

Joseph didn't even wait until they were out of the pen. Splat went the egg. And just in case Dad didn't notice, he announced it.

"I threw the egg down."

I thought Dad was going to turn purple.

"You threw it? On purpose?"

"I did, Dad. But I understand."

"You like broken eggs?"

"No, Dad. I understand."

"Well, if you like broken eggs, so much, then you can carry the broken egg!"

"No, Dad—I understand, I understand!" Joseph insisted.

But Dad wasn't listening. He took Joseph's hand and made him pick up what he could of the broken egg. Then he took Joseph's other hand and rubbed both his hands together in it.

"No!" Joseph was screaming. "I don't *want* to hold the broken egg! I don't *want* it all over my hands! It's yucky, Dad. I don't want it all over my hands!"

"Well, Buster, *I* don't want it all over the barn floor. Now do you understand?"

"I understand, Dad."

That was the fourth time Joseph tried to gather the eggs, and it was the day after open house.

The fifth time Joseph tried to gather the eggs was the next night.

"He's going to learn to bring in the eggs."

"John."

"Joseph, can you carry the egg?"

"I don't want to go to the barn."

"Can you carry the egg?"

"Yes, I can carry it."

"You won't break it?"

"I won't break it." He looked at Dad. "I won't. I'm big enough. I understand."

"Then come on. You're going to learn, if it takes me a dozen eggs to teach you."

I knew I was going, too. I couldn't miss out now. Besides, I wanted to see if Fluffy was making another nest. But I didn't know where Dad

113

was going to get a dozen eggs. The hens weren't laying that many—in fact, Mom had been buying extra eggs.

This time Joseph waited until they were out of the chicken pen. I guess he must have liked the splat on the bare cement better than the splat on the straw in the pen. But he did it—*splat*. He looked at me, and he looked at Dad and at the splat all over the floor.

If Dad turned purple that last time, I don't know what he turned this time. He was angry, all right. I don't know when I've ever seen him so angry before or since. In fact, he even scared me a little.

Without saying anything that I could understand, just sort of an "Aaaaaaaaagh!" Dad picked up the smashed egg and dumped it on top of Joseph's head.

"No. I understand, I understand! I won't do it again, Dad, I won't. I don't like egg on my hair. I understand! I don't like this! Not in my face and on my hair. I understand!"

There was one egg left, and Dad handed it to Joseph.

"This egg, I want for my breakfast."

But Joseph put his hands behind his back.

"No, I don't want to carry it."

Dad grabbed his hands and put the egg in it. "You *will* carry this to the house without breaking it, or it will be on your head with the other one. And we will practice until you *can* carry an egg inside. Do you understand that?"

"I understand. But I don't *like* egg in my hair."

"Let's go in to Mom."

I don't know if Dad remembered I was there or not, but I quickly shut the rabbit hutch and said good night to Fluffy, and followed.

The egg got to the kitchen.

Mom looked at Dad and at Joseph. Joseph's head was covered with egg. Egg yolk had dripped down his face and was starting to dry. Egg shell was mixed with the yolk in his hair and on his face. His eyes were still full of tears, and the dried tears had made streaks down his dirty cheeks mixed with the egg yolk.

"Here, Mommy," he said.

Mom looked at Dad again.

"That's my *big* boy," she said. "I *knew* you could bring in the eggs."

That was the fifth time Joseph tried to gather the eggs. After that time he never broke another egg on purpose. That was two days after open house.

# Chapter 10

Monday, I slipped into my seat at school before Richard and his watch arrived. *Maybe he's not coming today,* I thought. But that thought was short-lived because in another minute Richard sat down, too.

"How's the math whiz today?"

I decided to ignore him. But I did get out my math book instead of my library book. I opened it to the fractions and stared at the numbers. Why would anyone want to know how to write decimals as fractions, anyway?

"Your test is still on the board from open house," Richard pointed out.

He didn't need to tell me that. I knew it was still up there. I looked at the book. 9.05 = 9 5/100.

"Well, whiz, so's my spelling paper," Richard said.

"It is?" I knew what Richard's spelling papers looked like. They weren't any better than my math papers.

"It sure is. My mom and dad weren't happy either. Mom keeps telling me I should spell like you."

"How does she know how I spell?" Mrs. Rafferty hadn't bothered to put up my spelling papers.

"I told her."

"You told your mom I'm a good speller?" Why would he do something like that?

"Well..." For some reason Richard looked embarrassed. "How *do* you spell so good?"

"I don't know." That was the truth. I don't know why I know how to spell.

"Mom says you must study all the time."

"I don't study all the time." I thought of the times my math book had been closed while I read library books.

"Richard, you know I don't study. I don't even study when I'm supposed to."

"Then how do you do it? Why would anyone want to bother memorizing spelling anyway?"

Suddenly it hit me. "Tell me something, Richard. How do you know all about fractions and decimals? I was just wondering the very same thing about math. Who would want to change decimals to fractions?"

"I never memorize math. I just know it."

"But how? I never memorize spelling words, either."

"Really?"

"Sure. You know I read all the time. I just know how words are supposed to look. If I write it down, and it's spelled wrong, it looks wrong. But you can't tell a math problem by looking."

"No. But I don't remember not knowing how to add and subtract and even multiply. Dad and I always play math games."

"And I'm always reading. It's as simple as that."

"As what?"

"If you like something, it doesn't seem like work. Could you show me some math games? I know some library books you'd like—they're all about outer space."

"You mean there's books about it, not just movies?"

"And the books are always more exciting than the movies—the movies are too short."

"Okay. I'll show you some math puzzles."

But we couldn't start right then because the bell rang and Mrs. Rafferty was already telling us to be quiet.

"It's time to begin, class. Sheila, I wish you and Richard would spend your time more constructively. Neither one of you can afford to waste time talking."

I looked at Richard and grinned. She didn't realize we were talking about math and spelling.

Richard grinned back. Maybe he wasn't so bad, after all.

"It isn't funny, Sheila. Take out your math book and tell me how nine point zero five is written as a fraction."

"It's nine and five one hundreths. Nine with a five over one hundred."

Mrs. Rafferty looked at me, surprised. Her eyebrows shot up and her skinny little arm stopped in midair.

"Why, how did you know so quickly, Sheila?"

"I studied, Mrs. Rafferty."

"Well! I guess so. I knew if your parents saw your math papers, they'd see to it that you'd study."

Then I almost laughed out loud. I thought of everything that had happened since Thursday's open house. Joseph had torn up the room; Mom had read my rabbit story, and we'd left without even looking at the math test on the bulletin board or talking to Mrs. Rafferty. Joseph had learned to gather the eggs, and I could still see him with eggs dripping down his face, handing his egg to Mom while Mom told him he was a big boy.

Never once in that whole time had Mom or Dad said one thing about math. If they had seen the math test, they'd never said a thing about it. All Mom had ever said anything about was my story about Sandra and Snowball. Nothing about math.

This time I heard Richard chuckle. It wasn't a snicker. He wasn't making fun of me. He was laughing. Then I couldn't help it—I was laughing, too.

"Whatever is so funny, Sheila?" Mrs. Rafferty asked.

I knew I could never begin to explain what was so funny. I thought I had better not even try.

"It's just a great way to start the day, Mrs. Rafferty."

And do you know what? She smiled, too.

When I got home that night, I found Mom in the corner of the dining room with the glue in her hand doing something to the wallpaper.

"Hi, Mom."

"Hi, hon. Where's Jennifer?"

"Still coming up the lane. What are you doing?"

Mom took one of her big breaths. She looked kind of tired.

"I'm fixing the wallpaper."

"What happened?"

"Well, it got torn."

"It what?" I knew it had to be Joseph. "What did he do?"

"He opened the freezer and turned off the switch. That must have been last weekend when I saw him playing with the freezer door. I noticed the meat was getting soft when I took some out for supper. The power had been turned off, and

Joseph said he'd done it. When I put him in the corner to think about it, he tore off the wallpaper."

"Great. Where is he now?"

"He's in the laundry room. Sheila?"

"Yes."

"Don't say anything to Daddy about the wallpaper. The freezer's enough for one day."

"Okay."

I went into the laundry room and found Joseph sitting on top of the washing machine. He looked up at me and grinned, his dimples showing, and his big brown eyes looking bigger and browner than ever. I grinned back in spite of the wallpaper and the freezer. Then he put down the box of laundry detergent he had been playing with.

"Look, Sheila. I poured it all out," he announced.

And he had. A full box of laundry detergent had been poured into the washer.

"Joseph, you didn't!"

"I did."

I thought of Mom pasting the wallpaper back on the wall in the corner of the dining room. I thought of her asking me not to tell Dad because the freezer would be enough for one day. So I got a measuring cup and dipped all the detergent back into the box, one cup at a time.

"Sheila? What's going on?"

"Nothing, Mom," I said as I dipped. "I'm just keeping Joseph out of trouble." That was the truth, too. I knew I wouldn't tell Dad about the wallpaper, and I wouldn't tell Mom about the laundry detergent either.

When I finished, I said, "Come on, Joseph, let's go see Fluffy." Then I called to Mom, "Can I take Joseph with me to the barn?"

"Oh, Sheila, that would be such a help."

"Okay. See you later. Let's go, Joseph."

It was a beautiful October day. Jennifer and David were playing in the leaves, making leaf houses. The sun was shining, and there wasn't even one cloud in the sky—we couldn't have played cloud pictures if we had wanted to. It was still warm enough to be out without a jacket.

"We'll make leaf houses, too, Joseph, when we get back from the barn."

"Okay. Can I hold Alexander?"

"If you can catch him. But you can't chase the chickens."

"I won't chase the chickens, Sheila. I won't."

I didn't believe him, but I didn't think it mattered. I'd just be extra careful with the door to the chicken pen.

Joseph climbed the gate, and I swung it wide open so that he could pretend it was a horse, and pretty soon he was whinnying just like a horse. I'd like to have a real horse someday. Once when I asked Mom for a horse, she just laughed and said, "Who'd feed it, Sheila?" But I knew I would.

In the barnyard Joseph took off after Alex, and Alex waddled away quacking. Joseph had almost caught him when he did it again—he slipped in some sheep manure and fell down. But this time it stopped him for just a few seconds. He jumped up, took off after Alex, and caught him. I laughed.

"Look, Sheila, I have Alexander!"

"You sure do, Bud. You sure do. Let's go feed the rabbits."

The barn swallows had left for the winter, but the barn still had the nice smell of chickens, sheep, and rabbits. I could see the empty swallow nest where the young birds had left it, on a beam above Fluffy's hutch.

And in the hutch with Fluffy was a nest full of fur, and the fur was moving!

I took a deep breath, and as quietly as I could, I opened the hutch door and very carefully picked up the fur. There they were—four baby rabbits, all safe and warm. Just as carefully, I covered them up again, and as slowly and as quietly as I could, I filled Fluffy's water dish and her feed dish and shut the hutch door. Fluffy didn't jump once or seem at all scared.

I knew better than to tell Joseph just yet. I didn't want him screaming and scaring Fluffy again.

But they were there, four baby rabbits, and they were alive!

We got the eggs with Joseph carrying his all by himself. Then we went outside the barn, and closed the barn door. The whole time I was as quiet as I could be, and for some reason, Joseph stayed quiet, too, even if he didn't know about the baby rabbits.

I could see that Jennifer and David were still playing in the leaves by the house, so I said to Joseph, "Come on, I'll give you a ride on the gate, and we'll go play in the leaves."

He climbed up and whinnyed like a horse as I closed the gate.

*I would like a horse,* I thought. *And I would feed it every day.* I looked at Joseph, whinnying on the gate, and I knew I loved him. *But I guess I won't start praying for one right away.*

Susan Sommer was born and raised in Bluffton, Ohio, one of six children of Carl M. and
Sarah (Miller) Lehman. She grew up attending
First Mennonite Church in Bluffton, where she
became a member. She graduated from Bluffton
College with a Bachelor of Arts in English. Both
the church and the college have exerted a strong
influence in her life, Susan says.

She married James T. Sommer, and they
resided in Delphos, Ohio, for four years, where
they taught in the public schools. During that

time she studied fiction writing in a Master of Fine Arts program at Bowling Green State University in Ohio.

She and her husband currently live in central Illinois and are members of First Mennonite Church, Morton. They have four young children, one of whom is adopted.